DATE DUE

NOV 7 1979			
NOV 20 1979			
APR 24 1985			
May 22 1985			
JUN 04 1985 BR			

DEMCO 38-297

SCIENCE FICTION

This is a volume in the
Arno Press collection

SCIENCE FICTION

ADVISORY EDITORS

R. Reginald

Douglas Menville

See last pages of this volume
for a complete list of titles

The MAN WHO ROCKED THE EARTH

ARTHUR TRAIN
AND
ROBERT WILLIAMS WOOD

ARNO PRESS
A New York Times Company
New York — 1975

Reprint Edition 1974 by Arno Press Inc.

Copyright © 1915 by Doubleday, Page & Company

Reprinted by permission of Mrs. Robert W. Wood

Reprinted from a copy in The Library
of the University of California, Riverside

SCIENCE FICTION
ISBN for complete set: 0-405-06270-2
See last pages of this volume for titles.

Manufactured in the United States of America

Library of Congress Cataloging in Publication Data

Train, Arthur Cheney, 1875-1945.
  The man who rocked the earth.

  (Science fiction)
  Reprint of the ed. published by Doubleday, Page,
Garden City, N. Y.
  I. Wood, Robert Williams, 1868-1955, joint author.
II. Title. III. Series.
PZ3.T682Mak6 [PS3539.R23] 813'.5'2 74-16523
ISBN 0-405-06315-6

THE MAN WHO ROCKED
THE EARTH

"I thought, too, of the first and most significant realization which the reading of astronomy imposes: that of the exceeding delicacy of the world's position; how, indeed, we are dependent for life, and all that now is, upon the small matter of the tilt of the poles; and that we, as men, are products, as it were, not only of earth's precarious position, but of her more precarious tilt."

—W. L. Comfort, Nov., 1914

The
MAN WHO ROCKED THE EARTH

By ARTHUR TRAIN
AND
ROBERT WILLIAMS WOOD

Frontispiece

GARDEN CITY   NEW YORK
DOUBLEDAY, PAGE & COMPANY
1915

Copyright, 1915, *by*
DOUBLEDAY, PAGE & COMPANY

*All rights reserved, including that of
translation into foreign languages,
including the Scandinavian*

COPYRIGHT, 1914, 1915, THE CURTIS PUBLISHING CO.

THE MAN WHO ROCKED
THE EARTH

INSTANTLY THE EARTH BLEW UP LIKE A CANNON—UP INTO THE AIR, A THOUSAND MILES UP

The Man Who Rocked the Earth

PROLOGUE

BY JULY 1, 1916, the war had involved every civilized nation upon the globe except the United States of North and of South America, which had up to that time succeeded in maintaining their neutrality. Belgium, Holland, Denmark, Switzerland, Poland, Austria Hungary, Lombardy, and Servia, had been devastated. Five million adult male human beings had been exterminated by the machines of war, by disease, and by famine. Ten million had been crippled or invalided. Fifteen million women and children had been rendered widows or orphans. Industry there was none. No crops were harvested or sown. The ocean was devoid of sails. Throughout European Christendom women had taken the place of men as field hands, labourers, mechanics, merchants, and manufacturers. The amalgamated debt of the involved nations, amounting to more than $100,000,000,000, had bankrupted the world. Yet the starving armies continued to slaughter one another.

Siberia was a vast charnel-house of Tartars, Chinese, and Russians. Northern Africa was a holocaust. Within sixty miles of Paris lay an army of two million Germans, while three million Russians had invested Berlin. In Belgium an English army of eight hundred and fifty thousand men faced an equal force of Prussians and Austrians, neither daring to take the offensive.

The inventive genius of mankind, stimulated by the exigencies of war, had produced a multitude of death-dealing mechanisms, most of which had in turn been rendered ineffective by some counter-invention of another nation. Three of these products of the human brain, however, remained unneutralized and in large part accounted for the impasse at which the hostile armies found themselves. One of these had revolutionized warfare in the field, and the other two had destroyed those two most important factors of the preliminary campaign—the aeroplane and the submarine. The German dirigibles had all been annihilated within the first ten months of the war in their great cross-channel raid by Pathé contact bombs trailed at the ends of wires by high-flying French planes. This, of course, had from the beginning been confidently predicted by the French War Department. But by November, 1915, both the allied and the German aerial fleets had been wiped from the clouds by Federston's vortex guns, which by projecting a whirling ring of air to a height of over five thousand feet crumpled the craft in mid-sky like so many butterflies in a simoon.

The second of these momentous inventions was Captain Barlow's device for destroying the periscopes of submarines, thus rendering them blind and helpless. Once they were forced to the surface such craft were easily destroyed by gun fire or driven to a sullen refuge in protecting harbours.

The third, and perhaps the most vital, invention was Dufay's nitrogen-iodide pellets, which when sown by pneumatic guns upon the slopes of a battlefield, the ground outside intrenchments, or round the glacis of a fortification made approach by an attacking army impossible and the position impregnable. These pellets, only the size of No. 4 bird shot and harmless out of contact with air, became highly explosive two minutes after they had been scattered broadcast upon the soil, and any friction would discharge them with sufficient force to fracture or dislocate the bones of the human foot or to put out of service the leg of a horse. The victim attempting to drag himself away inevitably sustained further and more serious injuries, and no aid could be given to the injured, as it was impossible to reach them. A field well planted with such pellets was an impassable barrier to either infantry or cavalry, and thus any attack upon a fortified position was doomed to failure. By surprise alone could a general expect to achieve a victory. Offensive warfare had come almost to a standstill.

Germany had seized Holland, Denmark, and Switzerland. Italy had annexed Dalmatia and the Trentino; and a new Slav republic had arisen out of what had been Hungary, Croatia, Bosnia, Herzegovina, Servia, Roumania, Montenegro, Albania, and Bulgaria. Turkey had vanished from the map of Europe; while the United States of South America, composed of the Spanish-speaking South American Republics, had been formed. The mortality continued at an average of two thousand a day, of which

THE MAN WHO ROCKED THE EARTH

75 per cent. was due to starvation and the plague. Maritime commerce had ceased entirely, and in consequence of this the merchant ships of all nations rotted at the docks.

The Emperor of Germany, and the kings of England and of Italy, had all voluntarily abdicated in favour of a republican form of government. Europe and Asia had run amuck, hysterical with fear and blood. As well try to pacify a pack of mad and fighting dogs as these frenzied myriads with their half-crazed generals. They lay, these armies, across the fair bosom of the earth like dying monsters, crimson in their own blood, yet still able to writhe upward and deal death to any other that might approach. They were at a deadlock, yet each feared to make the first overtures for peace. There was, in actuality, no longer even an English or a German nation. It was an orgy of homicide, in which the best of mankind were wantonly destroyed, leaving only the puny, the feeble-minded, the deformed, and the ineffectual to perpetuate the race.

I

IT WAS three minutes past three postmeridian in the operating room of the new Wireless Station recently installed at the United States Naval Observatory at Georgetown. Bill Hood, the afternoon operator, was sitting in his shirt sleeves with his receivers at his ears, smoking a corncob pipe and awaiting a call from the flagship *Lincoln* of the North Atlantic Patrol with which, somewhere just off Hatteras, he had been in communication a few moments before. The air was quiet.

Hood was a fat man, and so of course good-natured; but he was serious about his work and hated all interfering amateurs. Of late these wireless pests had become particularly obnoxious, as practically everything was sent out in code and they had nothing with which to occupy themselves. But it was a hot day and none of them seemed to be at work. On one side of his desk a tall thermometer indicated that the temperature of the room was 91 degrees

THE MAN WHO ROCKED THE EARTH 9

Fahrenheit; on the other a big clock, connected with some extraneous mechanism by a complicated system of brass rods and wires, ticked off the minutes and seconds with a peculiar metallic self-consciousness, as if aware of its own importance in being the official timepiece, as far as there was an official timepiece, for the entire United States of America.

Hood from time to time tested his converters and detector, and then resumed his non-official study of the adventures of a great detective who pursued the baffling criminal by the aid of all the latest scientific discoveries. Hood thought it was good stuff, although at the same time he knew, of course, that it was rot. He was a practical man of little imagination, and, though the detective did not interest him particularly, he liked the scientific part of the stories. He was thrifty, of Scotch-Irish descent, and at two minutes past three had never had an adventure in his life. At three minutes past three he began his career as one of the celebrities of the world.

As the minute hand of the official clock dropped into its slot somebody called the Naval Observatory. The call was so faint as to be barely audible, in spite of the fact that Hood's instrument was tuned for a three-thousand-metre wave. Supposing quite naturally that the person calling had a shorter wave, he gradually cut out the inductance of his receiver; but the sound faded out entirely, and he returned to his original inductance and shunted in his condenser, upon which the call immediately increased in volume. Evidently the other chap was using a big wave, bigger than Georgetown.

Hood puckered his brows and looked about him. Lying on a shelf above his instrument was one of the new ballast coils that Henderson had used with the long waves from lightning flashes, and he leaned over and connected the heavy spiral of closely wound wire, throwing it into his circuit. Instantly the telephones spoke so loud that he could hear the shrill cry of the spark even from where the receivers lay beside him on the table. Quickly fastening them to his ears he listened. The sound was clear, sharp, and metallic, and vastly higher in pitch than a ship's call. It couldn't be the *Lincoln*.

"By gum!" muttered Hood. "That fellow must have a twelve-thousand-metre wave length with fifty kilowatts behind it, sure! There ain't another station in the world but this can pick him up!"

"NAA—NAA—NAA," came the call.

Throwing in his rheostat he sent an "O.K" in reply, and waited expectantly, pencil in hand. A moment more and he dropped his pencil in disgust.

"Just another bug!" he remarked aloud to the thermometer. "Ought to be poisoned! What a whale of a wave length, though!"

For several minutes he listened intently, for the amateur was sending insistently, repeating everything twice as if he meant business.

"He's a jolly joker all right," muttered Hood, this time to the clock. "Must be pretty hard up for something to do!"

Then he laughed out loud and took up the pencil again. This amateur, whoever he was, was almost as good as his detective story. The "bug" called the Naval Observatory once more and began repeating his entire message for the third time.

"To all mankind"—he addressed himself modestly—"To all mankind—To all mankind—I am the dictator—of human destiny—Through the earth's rotation—I control—day and night—summer and winter—I command the—cessation of hostilities and—the abolition of war upon the globe—I appoint the

—United States—as my agent for this purpose—As evidence of my power I shall increase the length of the day—from midnight to midnight—of Thursday, July 22d, by the period of five minutes.—Pax."

The jolly joker, having repeated thus his extraordinary message to all mankind, stopped sending.

"Well, I'll be hanged!" gasped Bill Hood. Then he wound up his magnetic detector and sent an answering challenge into the ether.

"Can—the—funny—stuff!" he snapped. "And tune out—or—we'll revoke—your license!"

"What a gall!" he grunted, folding up the yellow sheet of pad paper upon which he had taken down the message to all mankind and thrusting it into his book for a marker. "All the fools aren't dead yet!"

Then he picked up the *Lincoln* and got down to real work. The "bug" and his message passed from memory.

II

THE following Thursday afternoon a perspiring and dusty stranger from St. Louis, who, with the Metropolitan Art Museum as his objective, was trudging wearily through Central Park, New York City, at two o'clock, paused to gaze with some interest at the obelisk known as Cleopatra's Needle. The heat rose in shimmering waves from the asphalt of the roadway, but the stranger was used to heat and he was conscientiously engaged in the duty of seeing New York. Opposite the Museum he seated himself upon a bench in the shade of a faded dogwood and wiped the moisture from his eyes. The glare from the unprotected boulevards was terrific. Under these somewhat unfavourable conditions he was occupied in studying the monument of Egypt's past magnificence when he felt a slight dragging sensation. It was indefinable and had no visual concomitant. But it was as though the brakes were being gently applied to a Pullman train. He was the only human being in the neighbourhood; not even a policeman was visible; and the experience gave him a creepy feeling. Then to his amazement Cleopatra's Needle slowly toppled from its pedestal and fell with a crash across the roadway. At first he thought it an optical illusion and wiped his eyes again, but it was nothing of the kind. The monument, which had a moment before pointed to the zenith, now lay shattered in three pieces upon the softening concrete of the drive. The stranger arose and examined the fragments of the monolith, one of which lay squarely across the road, barring all passage. Round the pedestal were scattered small pieces of broken granite, and from these, after looking about cautiously, he chose one with care and placed it in his pocket.

"Gosh!" he whispered to himself as he hurried toward Fifth Avenue. "That'll just be something to tell 'em at home! Eh, Bill?"

The dragging sensation experienced by the tourist from St. Louis was felt by many millions of people all over the world, but, as in most countries it occurred coincidently with pronounced earthquake shocks and tremblings, for the most part it passed unnoticed as a specific, individual phenomenon.

Hood, in the wireless room at Georgetown, suddenly heard in his receivers a roar like that of Niagara and quickly removed them from his ears. He had never known such statics. He was familiar with electrical disturbances in the ether, but this was beyond anything in his experience. Moreover, when he next tried to use his instruments he discovered that something had put the whole apparatus out of commission. About an hour later he felt a pronounced pressure in his eardrums, which gradually passed off. The wireless refused to work for nearly eight hours, and it was still recalcitrant when he went off duty at seven o'clock. He had not felt the quivering of the earth round Washington, and being an unimaginative man he accepted the other facts of the situation philosophically. The statics would pass, and then Georgetown would be in communication with the rest of the world again, that was all. At seven o'clock the night shift came in, and Hood borrowed a pipeful of tobacco from him and put on his coat.

"Say, Bill, did you feel the shock?" asked the shift, hanging up his hat and taking a match from Hood.

"No," answered the latter, "but the statics have

put the machine on the blink. She'll come round all right in an hour or so. The air's gummy with ions. Shock, did you say?"

"Sure. Had 'em all over the country. Say, the boys at the magnetic observatory claim their compass shifted east and west instead of north and south, and stayed that way for five minutes. Didn't you feel the air pressure? I should worry! And say, I just dropped into the Meteorological Department's office and looked at the barometer. She'd jumped up half an inch in about two seconds, wiggled round some, and then come back to normal. You can see the curve yourself if you ask Fraser to show you the self-registering barograph. Some doin's, I tell you!"

He nodded his head with an air of importance.

"Take your word for it," answered Hood without emotion, save for a slight annoyance at the other's arrogation of superior information. "'Tain't the first time there's been an earthquake since creation." And he strolled out, swinging to the doors behind him.

The night shift settled himself before the instruments with a look of dreary resignaton.

"Say," he muttered aloud, "you couldn't jar that

feller with a thirteen-inch bomb! He wouldn't even rub himself!"

Hood, meantime, bought an evening paper and walked slowly to the district where he lived. It was a fine night and there was no particular excitement in the streets. His wife opened the door.

"Well," she greeted him, "I'm glad you've come home at last. I was plumb scared something had happened to you. Such a shaking and rumbling and rattling I never did hear! Did you feel it?"

"I didn't feel nothin'!" answered Bill Hood. "Some one said there was a shock, that was all I heard about it. The machine's out of kilter."

"They won't blame you, will they?" she asked anxiously.

"You bet they won't!" he replied. "Look here, I'm hungry. Are the waffles ready?"

"Have 'em in a jiffy!" she smiled. "You go in and read your paper."

He did as he was directed, and seated himself in a rocker under the gaslight. After perusing the baseball news he turned back to the front page. The paper was a fairly late edition, containing up-to-the-minute telegraphic notes. In the centre column, alongside the announcement of the annihilation of three entire regiments of Silesians by the explosion of nitroglycerine concealed in dummy gun carriages, was the following:

CLEOPATRA'S NEEDLE FALLS

Earthquake Destroys Famous Monument
Shocks Felt Here and All Over U. S.

Washington was visited by a succession of earthquake shocks early this afternoon, which, in varying force, were felt throughout the United States and Europe. Little damage was done, but those having offices in tall buildings had an unpleasant experience which they will not soon forget. A peculiar phenomenon accompanying this seismic disturbance was the variation of the magnetic needle by over eighty degrees from north to east and an extraordinary rise and fall of the barometer. All wireless communication had to be abandoned, owing to the ionizing of the atmosphere, and up to the time this edition went to press had not been resumed. Telegrams by way of Colon report similar disturbances in South America. In New York the monument in Central Park known as Cleopatra's Needle was thrown from its pedestal and broken into three pieces. The contract for its repair and replacement has already been let. The famous monument was a present from the Khedive of Egypt to the United States, and formerly stood in Alexandria. The late William

THE MAN WHO ROCKED THE EARTH 19

H. Vanderbilt defrayed the expense of transporting it to this country.

Bill Hood read this with scant interest. The Giants had knocked the Braves' pitcher out of the box, and an earthquake seemed a small matter. His mind did not once revert to the mysterious message from Pax the day before. He was thinking of something far more important.

"Say, Nellie," he demanded, tossing aside the paper impatiently, "ain't those waffles ready yet?"

III

ON THAT same evening, Thursday, July 22d, two astronomers attached to the Naval Observatory sat in the half darkness of the meridian-circle room watching the firmament sweep slowly across the aperture of the giant lens. The chamber was as quiet as the grave, the two men rarely speaking as they noted their observations. Paris might be taken, Berlin be razed, London put to the torch; a million human beings might be blown into eternity, or the shrieks of mangled creatures lying in heaps before pellet-strewn barbed-wire entanglements rend the summer night; great battleships of the line might plunge to the bottom, carrying their crews with them; and the dead of two continents rot unburied—yet unmoved the stars would pursue their nightly march across the heavens, cruel day would follow pitiless night, and the careless earth follow its accustomed orbit as though the race were not writhing in its death agony. Gazing into the infinity of space human existence seemed but the scum upon a rainpool, human warfare but the frenzy of insectivora. Unmindful of the starving hordes of Paris and Berlin, of plague-swept Russia, or of the drowned thousands of the North Baltic Fleet, these two men calmly studied the procession of the stars—the onward bore of the universe through space, and the spectra of newborn or dying worlds.

It was a suffocatingly hot night and their foreheads reeked with sweat. Dim shapes on the walls of the room indicated what by day was a tangle of clockwork and recording instruments, connected by electricity with various buttons and switches upon the table. The brother of the big clock in the wireless operating room hung nearby, its face illuminated by a tiny electric lamp, showing the hour to be eleven-fifty. Occasionally the younger man made a remark in a low tone, and the elder wrote something on a card.

"The 'seeing' is poor to-night," said Evarts, the younger man. "The upper air is full of striae and, though it seems like a clear night, everything looks dim—a volcanic haze probably. Perhaps the Aleutian Islands are in eruption again."

"Very likely," answered Thornton, the elder astronomer. "The shocks this afternoon would indicate something of the sort."

"Curious performance of the magnetic needle. They say it held due east for several minutes," continued Evarts, hoping to engage his senior in conversation—almost an impossibility, as he well knew.

Thornton did not reply. He was carefully observing the infinitesimal approach of a certain star to the meridian line, marked by a thread across the circle's aperture. When that point of light should cross the thread it would be midnight, and July 22, 1916, would be gone forever. Every midnight the indicating stars crossed the thread exactly on time, each night a trifle earlier than the night before by a definite and calculable amount, due to the march of the earth around the sun. So they had crossed the lines in every observatory since clocks and telescopes had been invented. Heretofore, no matter what cataclysm of nature had occurred, the star had always crossed the line not a second too soon or a second too late, but exactly on time. It was the one positively predictable thing, foretellable for ten or for ten thousand years by a simple mathematical calculation. It was surer than death or the taxman. It was absolute.

Thornton was a reserved man of few words—impersonal, methodical, serious. He spent many nights there with Evarts, hardly exchanging a phrase with him, and then only on some matter immediately concerned with their work. Evarts could dimly see his long, grave profile bending over his eyepiece, shrouded in the heavy shadows across the table. He felt a great respect, even tenderness, for this taciturn, high-principled, devoted scientist. He had never seen him excited, hardly ever aroused. He was a man of figures, whose only passion seemed to be the "music of the spheres."

A long silence followed, during which Thornton seemed to bend more intently than ever over his eyepiece. The hand of the big clock slipped gradually to midnight.

"There's something wrong with the clock," said Thornton suddenly, and his voice sounded curiously dry, almost unnatural. "Telephone to the equatorial room for the time."

Puzzled by Thornton's manner Evarts did as instructed.

"Forty seconds past midnight," came the reply from the equatorial observer.

Evarts repeated the answer for Thornton's benefit, looking at their own clock at the same time. It pointed to exactly forty seconds past the hour. He heard Thornton suppress something like an oath.

"There's something the matter!" repeated Thornton dumbly. "Aeta isn't within five minutes of crossing. Both clocks can't be wrong!"

He pressed a button that connected with the wireless room.

"What's the time?" he called sharply through the nickel-plated speaking-tube.

"Forty-five seconds past the hour," came the answer. Then: "But I want to see you, sir. There's something queer going on. May I come in?"

"Come!" almost shouted Thornton.

A moment later the flushed face of Williams, the night operator, appeared in the doorway.

"Excuse me, sir," he stammered, "but something fierce must have happened! I thought you ought to know. The Eiffel Tower has been trying to talk to us for over two hours, but I can't get what he's saying."

"What's the matter—atmospherics?" snapped Evarts.

"No; the air *was* full of them, sir—shrieking with them you might say; but they've stopped now. The trouble has been that I've been jammed by the Brussels station talking to the Belgian Congo—same wave length—and I couldn't tune Brussels out. Every once in a while I'd get a word of what Paris was saying, and it's always the same word—'*heure.*' But just now Brussels stopped sending and I got the complete message of the Eiffel Tower. They wanted to know our time by Greenwich. I gave it to 'em. Then Paris said to tell you to take your transit with great care and send result to them immediately——"

The ordinarily calm Thornton gave a great suspiration and his face was livid. "Aeta's just crossed —we're five minutes out! Evarts, am I crazy? Am I talking straight?"

Evarts laid his hand on the other's arm.

"The earthquake's knocked out your transit," he suggested.

"And Paris—how about Paris?" asked Thornton. He wrote something down on a card mechanically and started for the door. "Get me the Eiffel Tower!" he ordered Williams.

The three men stood motionless, as the wireless man sent the Eiffel Tower call hurtling across the Atlantic:

"ETA—ETA—ETA."

"All right," whispered Williams, "I've got 'em."

"Tell Paris that our clocks are all out five minutes according to the meridian."

Williams worked the key rapidly, and then listened.

"The Eiffel Tower says that their chronometers also appear to be out by the same time, and that Greenwich and Moscow both report the same thing. Wait a minute! He says Moscow has wired that at eight o'clock last evening a tremendous aurora of bright yellow light was seen to the northwest, and that their spectroscopes showed the helium line only. He wants to know if we have any explanation to offer——"

"Explanation!" gasped Evarts. "Tell Paris that we had earthquake shocks here together with violent seismic movements, sudden rise in barometer, followed by fall, statics, and erratic variation in the magnetic needle."

"What does it all mean?" murmured Thornton, staring blankly at the younger man.

The key rattled and the rotary spark whined into a shriek. Then silence.

"Paris says that the same manifestations have been observed in Russia, Algeria, Italy, and London," called out Williams. "Ah! What's that? Nauen's calling." Again he sent the blue flame crackling between the coils. "Nauen reports an error of five minutes in their meridian observations according to the official clocks. And hello! He says Berlin has capitulated and that the Russians began marching through at daylight—that is about two hours ago. He says he is about to turn the station over to the Allied Commissioners, who will at once assume charge."

Evarts whistled.

"How about it?" he asked of Thornton.

The latter shook his head gravely.

"It may be—explainable—or," he added hoarsely, "it may mean the end of the world."

Williams sprang from his chair and confronted Thornton.

"What do you mean?" he almost shouted.

"Perhaps the universe is running down!" said Evarts soothingly. "At any rate, keep it to yourself, old chap. If the jig is up there's no use scaring people to death a month or so too soon!"

Thornton grasped an arm of each.

"Not a word of this to anybody!" he ground out through compressed lips. "Absolute silence, or hell may break loose on earth!"

IV

FREE translation of the Official Report of the Imperial Commission of the Berlin Academy of Science to the Imperial Commissioners of the German Federated States:

"The unprecedented cosmic phenomena which occurred on the 22d and 27th days of the month of July, and which were felt over the entire surface of the globe, have left a permanent effect of such magnitude on the position of the earth's axis in space and the duration of the period of the rotation, that it is impossible to predict at the present time the ultimate changes or modifications in the climatic conditions which may follow. This commission has considered most carefully the possible causes that may have been responsible for this catastrophe—(*Weltunfall*)—and, by eliminating every hypothesis that was incapable of explaining all of the various disturbances, is now in a position to present two theories, either one of which appears to be capable of explaining the recent disturbances.

"The phenomena in question may be briefly summarized as follows;

"1. THE YELLOW AURORA. In Northern Europe this appeared suddenly on the night of July 22d as a broad, faint sheaf—(*Lichtbündel*)—of clear yellow light in the western sky. Reports from America show that at Washington it appeared in the north as a narrow shaft of light, inclined at an angle of about thirty degrees with the horizon, and shooting off to the east. Near the horizon it was extremely brilliant, and the spectroscope showed that the light was due to glowing helium gas.

"The Potsdam Observatory reported that the presence of sodium has been detected in the aurora; but this appears to have been a mistake due to the faintness of the light and the circumstance that no comparison spectrum was impressed on the plate. On the photograph made at the Washington Observatory the helium line is certain, as a second exposure was made with a sodium flame; and the two lines are shown distinctly separated.

"2. THE NEGATIVE ACCELERATION. This phenomenon was observed to a greater or less extent all over the globe. It was especially marked near the equator; but in Northern Europe it was noted by only a few observers, though many clocks were stopped and other instruments deranged. There appears to be no doubt that a force of terrific magnitude was applied in a tangential direction to the surface of the earth, in such a direction as to oppose its axial rotation, with the effect that the surface velocity was diminished by about one part in three hundred, resulting in a lengthening of the day by five minutes, thirteen and a half seconds.

"The application of this brake—(*Bremsekraft*), as we may term it—caused acceleration phenomena to

THE MAN WHO ROCKED THE EARTH 31

manifest themselves precisely as on a railroad train when being brought to a stop. The change in the surface speed of the earth at the equator has amounted to about 6.4 kilometres an hour; and various observations show that this change of velocity was brought about by the operation of the unknown force for a period of time of less than three minutes. The negative acceleration thus represented would certainly be too small to produce any marked physiological sensations, and yet the reports from various places indicate that they were certainly observed. The sensations felt are usually described as similar to those experienced in a moving automobile when the brake is very gently applied.

"Moreover, certain destructive actions are reported from localities near the equator—chimneys fell and tall buildings swayed; while from New York comes the report that the obelisk in Central Park was thrown from its pedestal. It appears that these effects were due to the circumstance that the alteration of velocity was propagated through the earth as a wave similar to an earthquake wave, and that the effects were cumulative at certain points—a theory that is substantiated by reports that at certain localities, even near the equator, no effects were noted.

"3. TIDAL WAVES. These were observed everywhere and were very destructive in many places. In the Panama Canal, which is near the equator and which runs nearly east and west, the sweep of the water was so great that it flowed over the Gatun Lock. On the eastern coasts of the various continents there was a recession of the sea, the fall of the tide being from three to five metres below the low-water mark. On the western coasts there was a corresponding rise, which in some cases reached a level of over twelve metres.

"That the tidal phenomena were not more marked and more destructive is a matter of great surprise, and has been considered as evidence that the retarding force was not applied at a single spot on the earth's surface, but was a distributed force, which acted on the water as well as on the land, though to a less extent. It is difficult, however, to conceive of a force capable of acting in such a way; and Björnson's theory of the magnetic vortex in the ether has been rejected by this commission.

"4. ATMOSPHERIC DISTURBANCES. Some time after the appearance of the yellow aurora a sudden rise in atmospheric pressure, followed by a gradual fall considerably below the normal pressure, was recorded over the entire surface of the globe. Calculations based on the time of arrival of this disturbance at widely separated points show that it proceeded with the velocity of sound from a point situated probably in Northern Labrador. The maximum rise of pressure recorded was registered at Halifax, the self-recording barographs showing that the pressure rose over six centimetres in less than five minutes.

"5. SHIFT IN DIRECTION OF THE EARTH'S AXIS. The axis of the earth has been shifted in space by the disturbance and now points almost exactly toward the double star Delta Ursæ Minoris. This change appears to have resulted from the circumstance that the force was applied to the surface of the globe in a direction not quite parallel to the direction of rotation, the result being the development of a new axis and a shift in the positions of the poles, which it will now be necessary to rediscover.

"It appears that these most remarkable cosmic phenomena can be explained in either of two ways: they may have resulted from an explosive or volcanic discharge from the surface of the earth, or from the oblique impact of a meteoric stream moving at a very high velocity. It seems unlikely that sufficient energy to bring about the observed changes could have been developed by a volcanic disturbance of the ordinary type; but if radioactive forces are allowed to come into play the amount of energy available is practically unlimited.

"It is difficult, however, to conceive of any way in which a sudden liberation of atomic energy could have been brought about by any terrestrial agency; so that the first theory, though able to account for the facts, seems to be the less tenable of the two. The meteoric theory offers no especial difficulty. The energy delivered by a comparatively small mass of finely divided matter, moving at a velocity of several hundred kilometres a second—and such a velocity is by no means unknown—would be amply sufficient to alter the velocity of rotation by the small amount observed.

"Moreover, the impact of such a meteoric stream may have developed a temperature sufficiently high to bring about radioactive changes, the effect of which would be to expel helium and other disintegration products at cathode-ray velocity—(*Kathoden-Strahlen-Fortpflanzung-Geschwindigkeit*)—from the surface of the earth; and the recoil exerted by this expulsion would add itself to the force of the meteoric impact.

"The presence of helium makes this latter hypothesis not altogether improbable, while the atmospheric wave of pressure would result at once from the disruption of the air by the passage of the meteor stream through it. Exploration of the region in which it seems probable that the disturbance took place will undoubtedly furnish the data necessary for the complete solution of the problem." [Pp. 17-19.]

V

AT TEN o'clock one evening, shortly after the occurrences heretofore described, an extraordinary conference occurred at the White House, probably the most remarkable ever held there or elsewhere. At the long table at which the cabinet meetings took place sat six gentlemen in evening dress, each trying to appear unconcerned, if not amused. At the head of the table was the President of the United States; next to him Count von Koenitz, the German Ambassador, representing the Imperial* German Commissioners, who had taken over the reins of the German Government after the abdication of the Kaiser; and, on the opposite side, Monsieur Emil Liban, Prince Rostoloff, and Sir John Smith, the respective ambassadors of France, Russia, and Great Britain. The sixth person was Thornton, the astronomer.

---

*The Germans were unwilling to surrender the use of the words "Empire" and "Imperial," even after they had adopted a republican form of government.

The President had only succeeded in bringing this conference about after the greatest effort and the most skilful diplomacy—in view of the extreme importance which, he assured them all, he attached to the matters which he desired to lay before them. Only for this reason had the ambassadors of warring nations consented to meet—unofficially as it were.

"With great respect, your Excellency," said Count von Koenitz, "the matter is preposterous—as much so as a fairy tale by Grimm! This wireless operator of whom you speak is lying about these messages. If he received them at all—a fact which hangs solely upon his word—he received them *after* and not *before* the phenomena recorded."

The President shook his head. "That might hold true of the first message—the one received July 19th," said he, "but the second message, foretelling the lengthening of July 27th, *was delivered on that day, and was in my hands before the disturbances occurred.*"

Von Koenitz fingered his moustache and shrugged his shoulders. It was clear that he regarded the whole affair as absurd, undignified.

Monsieur Liban turned impatiently from him.

"Your Excellency," he said, addressing the President, "I cannot share the views of Count von Koenitz. I regard this affair as of the most stupendous importance. Messages or no messages, extraordinary natural phenomena are occurring which may shortly end in the extinction of human life upon the planet. A power which can control the length of the day can annihilate the globe."

"You cannot change the facts," remarked Prince Rostoloff sternly to the German Ambassador. "The earth has changed its orbit. Professor Vaskofsky, of the Imperial College, has so declared. There is some cause. Be it God or devil, there is a cause. Are we to sit still and do nothing while the globe's crust freezes and our armies congeal into corpses?" He trembled with agitation.

"Calm yourself, *mon cher Prince!*" said Monsieur Liban. "So far we have gained fifteen minutes and have lost nothing! But, as you say, whether or not the sender of these messages is responsible, there is a cause, and we must find it."

"But how? That is the question," exclaimed the President almost apologetically, for he felt, as did Count von Koenitz, that somehow an explanation would shortly be forthcoming that would make this conference seem the height of the ridiculous. "I have already," he added hastily, "instructed the entire force of the National Academy of Sciences to direct its energies toward the solution of these phenomena. Undoubtedly Great Britain, Russia, Germany, and France are doing the same. The scientists report that the yellow aurora seen in the north, the earthquakes, the variation of the compass, and the eccentricities of the barometer are probably all connected more or less directly with the change in the earth's orbit. But they offer no explanation. They do not suggest what the aurora is nor why its appearance should have this effect. It, therefore, seems to me clearly my duty to lay before you all the facts as far as they are known to me. Among these facts are the mysterious messages received by wireless at the Naval Observatory immediately preceding these events."

"*Post hoc, ergo propter hoc!*" half sneered Von Koenitz.

The President smiled wearily.

"What do you wish me to do?" he asked, glancing round the table. "Shall we remain inactive? Shall we wait and see what may happen?"

"No! No!" shouted Rostoloff, jumping to his feet. "Another week and we may all be plunged into eternity. It is suicidal not to regard this matter seriously. We are sick from war. And perhaps Count von Koenitz, in view of the fall of Berlin, would welcome something of the sort as an honourable way out of his country's difficulties."

"Sir!" cried the count, leaping to his feet. "Have a care! It has cost Russia four million men to reach Berlin. When we have taken Paris we shall recapture Berlin and commence the march of our victorious eagles toward Moscow and the Winter Palace."

"Gentlemen! Gentlemen! Be seated, I implore you!" exclaimed the President.

The Russian and German ambassadors somewhat ungraciously resumed their former places, casting at each other glances of undisguised contempt.

"As I see the matter," continued the President, "there are two distinct propositions before you: The first relates to how far the extraordinary events of the past week are of such a character as to demand joint investigation and action by the Powers. The second involves the cause of these events and their connection with and relation to the sender of the messages signed Pax. I shall ask you to signify your opinion as to each of these questions."

"I believe that some action should be taken, based on the assumption that they are manifestations of one and the same power or cause," said Monsieur Liban emphatically.

"I agree with the French Ambassador," growled Rostoloff.

"I am of opinion that the phenomena should be the subject of proper scientific investigation," remarked Count von Koenitz more calmly. "But as far as these messages are concerned they are, if I may be pardoned for saying so, a foolish joke. It is undignified to take any cognizance of them."

"What do you think, Sir John?" asked the President, turning to the English Ambassador.

"Before making up my mind," returned the latter quietly, "I should like to see the operator who received them."

"By all means!" exclaimed Von Koenitz.

The President pressed a button and his secretary entered.

"I had anticipated such a desire on the part of all of you," he announced, "and arranged to have him here. He is waiting outside. Shall I have him brought in?"

"Yes! Yes!" answered Rostoloff. And the others nodded.

The door opened, and Bill Hood, wearing his best new blue suit and nervously twisting a faded bicycle cap between his fingers, stumbled awkwardly into the room. His face was bright red with embarrassment and one of his cheeks exhibited a marked protuberance. He blinked in the glare of the electric light.

"Mr. Hood," the President addressed him courteously, "I have sent for you to explain to these gentlemen, who are the ambassadors of the great European Powers, the circumstances under which you received the wireless messages from the unknown person describing himself as 'Pax.'"

Hood shifted from his right to his left foot and pressed his lips together. Von Koenitz fingered the waxed ends of his moustache and regarded the operator whimsically.

"In the first place," went on the President, "we desire to know whether the messages which you have reported were received under ordinary or under unusual conditions. In a word, could you form any opinion as to the whereabouts of the sender?"

Hood scratched the side of his nose in a manner politely doubtful.

"Sure thing, your Honour," he answered at last. "Sure the conditions was unusual. That feller has some juice and no mistake."

"Juice?" inquired Von Koenitz.

"Yare—current. Whines like a steel top. Fifty kilowatts sure, and maybe more! And a twelve-thousand-metre wave."

"I do not fully understand," interjected Rostoloff. "Please explain, sir."

"Ain't nothin' to explain," returned Hood. "He's just got a hell of a wave length, that's all. Biggest on earth. We're only tuned for a three-thousand-metre wave. At first I could hardly take him at all. I had to throw in our new Henderson ballast coils before I could hear properly. I reckon there ain't another station in Christendom can get him."

"Ah," remarked Von Koenitz. "One of your millionaire amateurs, I suppose."

"Yare," agreed Hood. "I thought sure he was a nut."

"A what?" interrupted Sir John Smith.

"A nut," answered Hood. "A crank, so to speak."

"Ah, 'krank'!" nodded the German. "Exactly—a lunatic! That is precisely what I say!"

"But I don't think it's no nut now," countered Hood valiantly. "If he is a bug he's the biggest bug in all creation, that's all I can say. He's got the goods, that's what he's got. He'll do some damage before he gets through."

"Are these messages addressed to anybody in particular?" inquired Sir John, who was studying Hood intently.

"Well, they are and they ain't. Pax—that's what he calls himself—signals NAA, our number, you understand, and then says what he has to say to the whole world, care of the United States. The first message I thought was a joke and stuck it in a book I was reading, '*Silas Snooks*'——"

"What?" ejaculated Von Koenitz impatiently.

"Snooks—man's name—feller in the book—nothing to do with this business," explained the operator. "I forgot all about it. But after the earthquake and all the rest of the fuss I dug it out and gave it to Mr. Thornton. Then on the 27th came the next one, saying that Pax was getting tired of waiting for us and was going to start something. That came at one o'clock in the afternoon, and the fun began at three sharp. The whole observatory went on the blink. Say, there ain't any doubt in your minds that it's *him*, is there?"

Von Koenitz looked cynically round the room.

"There is not!" exclaimed Rostoloff and Liban in the same breath.

The German laughed.

"Speak for yourselves, Excellencies," he sneered. His tone nettled the wireless representative of the sovereign American people.

"Do you think I'm a liar?" he demanded, clenching his jaw and glaring at Von Koenitz.

The German Ambassador shrugged his shoulders again. Such things were impossible in a civilized country—at Potsdam—but what could you expect——

"Steady, Hood!" whispered Thornton.

"Remember, Mr. Hood, that you are here to answer our questions," said the President sternly. "You must not address his Excellency, Baron von Koenitz, in this fashion."

THE MAN WHO ROCKED THE EARTH 45

"But the man was making a monkey of me!" muttered Hood. "All I say is, look out. This Pax is on his job and means business. I just got another call before I came over here—at nine o'clock."

"What was its purport?" inquired the President.

"Why, it said Pax was getting tired of nothing being done and wanted action of some sort. Said that men were dying like flies, and he proposed to put an end to it at any cost. And—and——"

"Yes! Yes!" ejaculated Liban breathlessly.

"And he would give further evidence of his control over the forces of nature to-night."

"Ha! Ha!" Von Koenitz leaned back in amusement. "My friend," he chuckled, "you—are—the 'nut'!"

What form Hood's resentment might have taken is problematical; but as the German's words left his mouth the electric lights suddenly went out and the windows rattled ominously. At the same moment each occupant of the room felt himself sway slightly toward the east wall, on which appeared a bright yellow glow. Instinctively they all turned to the window which faced the north. The whole sky was flooded with an orange-yellow aurora that rivalled the sunlight in intensity.

"What'd I tell you?" mumbled Hood.

The Executive Mansion quivered, and even in that yellow light the faces of the ambassadors seemed pale with fear. And then as the glow slowly faded in the north there floated down across the aperture of the window something soft and fluffy like feathers. Thicker and faster it came until the lawn of the White House was covered with it. The air in the room turned cold. Through the window a large flake circled and lit on the back of Rostoloff's head.

"Snow!" he cried. "A snowstorm—in August!"

The President arose and closed the window. Almost immediately the electric lights burned up again.

"Now are you satisfied?" cried Liban to the German.

"Satisfied?" growled Von Koenitz. "I have seen plenty of snowstorms in August. They have them daily in the Alps. You ask me if I am satisfied. Of what? That earthquakes, the aurora borealis, electrical disturbances, snowstorms exist—yes. That a mysterious bugaboo is responsible for these things—no!"

"What, then, do you require?" gasped Liban.

"More than a snowstorm!" retorted the German. "When I was a boy at the gymnasium we had a thunderstorm with fishes in it. They were everywhere one stepped, all over the ground. But we did not conclude that Jonah was giving us a demonstration of his power over the whale."

He faced the others defiantly; in his voice was mockery.

"You may retire, Mr. Hood," said the President. "But you will kindly wait outside."

"That is an honest man if ever I saw one, Mr. President," announced Sir John, after the operator had gone out. "I am satisfied that we are in communication with a human being of practically supernatural powers."

"What, then, shall be done?" inquired Rostoloff anxiously. "The world will be annihilated!"

"Your Excellencies"—Von Koenitz arose and took up a graceful position at the end of the table—"I must protest against what seems to me to be an extraordinary credulity upon the part of all of you.

I speak to you as a rational human being, not as an ambassador. Something has occurred to affect the earth's orbit. It may result in a calamity. None can foretell. This planet may be drawn off into space by the attraction of some wandering world that has not yet come within observation. But one thing we know: No power on or of the earth can possibly derange its relation to the other celestial bodies. That would be, as you say here, 'lifting one's self by one's own boot-straps.' I do not doubt the accuracy of your clocks and scientific instruments. Those of my own country are in harmony with yours. But to say that the cause of all this is a *man* is preposterous. If the mysterious Pax makes the heavens fall, they will tumble on his own head. Is he going to send himself to eternity along with the rest of us? Hardly! This Hood is a monstrous liar or a dangerous lunatic. Even if he has received these messages, they are the emanations of a crank, as, he says, he himself first suspected. Let us master this hysteria born of the strain of constant war. In a word, let us go to bed."

"Count von Koenitz," replied Sir John after a pause, "you speak forcefully, even persuasively. But your argument is based upon a proposition that is scientifically fallacious. An atom of gunpowder can disintegrate itself, 'lift itself by its own bootstraps!' Why not the earth? Have we as yet begun to solve all the mysteries of nature? Is it inconceivable that there should be an undiscovered explosive capable of disrupting the globe? We have earthquakes. Is it beyond imagination that the forces which produce them can be controlled?"

"My dear Sir John," returned Von Koenitz courteously, "my ultimate answer is that we have no adequate reason to connect the phenomena which have disturbed the earth's rotation with any human agency."

"That," interposed the President, "is something upon which individuals may well differ. I suppose that under other conditions you would be open to conviction?"

"Assuredly," answered Von Koenitz. "Should the sender of these messages prophesy the performance of some miracle that could not be explained by natural causes, I would be forced to admit my error."

Monsieur Liban had also arisen and was walking nervously up and down the room. Suddenly he turned to Von Koenitz and in a voice shaking with emotion cried: "Let us then invite Pax to give us a sign that will satisfy you."

"Monsieur Liban," replied Von Koenitz stiffly, "I refuse to place myself in the position of communicating with a lunatic."

"Very well," shouted the Frenchman, "I will take the responsibility of making myself ridiculous. I will request the President of the United States to act as the agent of France for this purpose."

He drew a notebook and a fountain pen from his pocket and carefully wrote out a message which he handed to the President. The latter read it aloud:

"*Pax:* The Ambassador of the French Republic requests me to communicate to you the fact that he desires some further evidence of your power to control the movements of the earth and the destinies of mankind, such phenomena to be preferably of a harmless character, but inexplicable by any theory of natural causation. I await your reply.
"THE PRESIDENT OF THE UNITED STATES.

"Send for Hood," ordered the President to the secretary who answered the bell. "Gentlemen, I suggest that we ourselves go to Georgetown and superintend the sending of this message."

THE MAN WHO ROCKED THE EARTH 51

Half an hour later Bill Hood sat in his customary chair in the wireless operating room surrounded by the President of the United States, the ambassadors of France, Germany, Great Britain, and Russia, and Professor Thornton. The faces of all wore expressions of the utmost seriousness, except that of Von Koenitz, who looked as if he were participating in an elaborate hoax. Several of these distinguished gentlemen had never seen a wireless apparatus before, and showed some excitement as Hood made ready to send the most famous message ever transmitted through the ether. At last he threw over his rheostat and the hum of the rotary spark rose into its staccato song. Hood sent out a few V's and then began calling:

"PAX—PAX—PAX."

Breathlessly the group waited while he listened for a reply. Again he called:

"PAX—PAX—PAX."

He had already thrown in his Henderson ballast coils and was ready for the now familiar wave. He closed his eyes, waiting for that sharp metallic cry that came no one knew whence. The others in the group also listened intently, as if by so doing they, too, might hear the answer if any there should be. Suddenly Hood stiffened.

"There he is!" he whispered. The President handed him the message, and Hood's fingers played over the key while the spark sent its singing note through the ether.

"Such phenomena to be preferably of a harmless character, but inexplicable by any theory of natural causation," he concluded.

An uncanny dread seized on Thornton, who had withdrawn himself into the background. What was this strange communion? Who was this mysterious Pax? Were these real men or creatures of a grotesque dream? Was he not drowsing over his eyepiece in the meridian-circle room? Then a simultaneous movement upon the part of those gathered round the operator convinced him of the reality of what was taking place. Hood was laboriously writing upon a sheet of yellow pad paper, and the ambassadors were unceremoniously crowding each other in their eagerness to read.

"To the President of the United States," wrote Hood: "In reply to your message requesting further evidence of my power to compel the cessation of hostilities within twenty-four hours, I"—there was a pause for nearly a minute, during which the ticking of the big clock sounded to Thornton like revolver shots—"I will excavate a channel through the Atlas Mountains and divert the Mediterranean into the Sahara Desert. PAX."

Silence followed the final transcription of the message from the unknown—a silence broken only by Bill Hood's tremulous, half-whispered: "He'll do it all right!"

Then the German Ambassador laughed.

"And thus save your ingenious nation a vast amount of trouble, Monsieur Liban," said he.

VI

A TRIPOLITAN fisherman, Mohammed Ben Ali el Bad, a holy man nearly seventy years of age, who had twice made the journey to Mecca and who now in his declining years occupied himself with reading the Koran and instructing his grandsons in the profession of fishing for mullet along the reefs of the Gulf of Cabes, had anchored for the night off the Tunisian coast, about midway between Sfax and Lesser Syrtis. The mullet had been running thick and he was well satisfied, for by the next evening he would surely complete his load and be able to return home to the house of his daughter, Fatima, the wife of Abbas, the confectioner. Her youngest son, Abdullah, a lithe lad of seventeen, was at that moment engaged in folding their prayer rugs, which had been spread in the bow of the falukah in order that they might have a clearer view as they knelt toward the Holy City. Chud, their slave, was cleaning mullet in the waist and chanting some weird song of his native land.

Mohammed Ben Ali el Bad was sitting cross-legged in the stern, smoking a hookah and watching the full moon sail slowly up above the Atlas Range to the southwest. The wind had died down and the sea was calm, heaving slowly with great orange-purple swells resembling watered silk. In the west still lingered the fast-fading afterglow, above which the stars glimmered faintly. Along the coast lights twinkled in scattered coves. Half a mile astern the Italian cruiser *Fiala* lay slowly swinging at anchor. From the forecastle came the smell of fried mullet. Mohammed Ben Ali was at peace with himself and with the world, including even the irritating Chud. The west darkened and the stars burned more brilliantly. With the hookah gurgling softly at his feet, Mohammed leaned back his head and gazed in silent appreciation at the wonders of the heavens. There was Turka Kabar, the crocodile; and Menish el Tabir, the sleeping beauty; and Rook Hamana, the leopard, and there—up there to the far north—was a shooting star. How gracefully it shot across the sky, leaving its wake of yellow light behind it! It was the season for shooting stars, he recollected. In an instant it would be gone—like a man's life! Saddened, he looked down at his hookah. When he should look up again—if in only an instant—the star would be gone. Presently he did look up again. But the star was still there, coming his way!

He rubbed his old eyes, keen as they were from habituation to the blinding light of the desert. Yes, the star was coming—coming fast.

"Abdullah!" he called in his high-pitched voice. "Chud! Come, see the star!"

Together they watched it sweep onward.

"By Allah! That is no star!" suddenly cried Abdullah. "It is an air-flying fire chariot! I can see it with my eyes—black, and spouting flames from behind."

"Black," echoed Chud gutturally. "Black and round! Oh, Allah!" He fell on his knees and knocked his head against the deck.

The star, or whatever it was, swung in a wide circle toward the coast, and Mohammed and Abdullah now saw that what they had taken to be a trail of fire behind was in fact a broad beam of yellow light that pointed diagonally earthward. It swept nearer and nearer, illuminating the whole sky and casting a shimmering reflection upon the waves.

THE MAN WHO ROCKED THE EARTH 57

A shrill whistle trilled across the water, accompanied by the sound of footsteps running along the decks of the cruiser. Lights flashed. Muffled orders were shouted.

"By the beard of the Prophet!" cried Mohammed Ali. "Something is going to happen!"

The small black object from which the incandescent beam descended passed at that moment athwart the face of the moon, and Abdullah saw that it was round and flat like a ring. The ray of light came from a point directly above it, passing through its aperture downward to the sea.

"Boom!" The fishing-boat shook to the thunder of the *Fiala's* eight-inch gun, and a blinding spurt of flame leaped from the cruiser's bows. With a whining shriek a shell rose toward the moon. There was a quick flash followed by a dull concussion. The shell had not reached a tenth of the distance to the flying machine.

And then everything happened at once. Mohammed described afterward to a gaping multitude of dirty villagers, while he sat enthroned upon his daughter's threshold, how the star-ship had sailed across the face of the moon and come to a standstill above the mountains, with its beam of yellow light pointing directly downward so that the coast could be seen bright as day from Sfax to Cabes. He saw, he said, genii climbing up and down on the beam. Be that as it may, he swears upon the Beard of the Prophet that a second ray of light—of a lavender colour, like the eye of a long-dead mullet—flashed down alongside the yellow beam. Instantly the earth blew up like a cannon—up into the air, a thousand miles up. It was as light as noonday. Deafened by titanic concussions he fell half dead. The sea boiled and gave off thick clouds of steam through which flashed dazzling discharges of lightning accompanied by a thundering, grinding sound like a million mills. The ocean heaved spasmodically and the air shook with a rending, ripping noise, as if Nature were bent upon destroying her own handiwork. The glare was so dazzling that sight was impossible. The falukah was tossed this way and that, as if caught in a simoon, and he was rolled hither and yon in the company of Chud, Abdullah, and the headless mullet.

This earsplitting racket continued, he says, without interruption for two days. Abdullah says it was several hours; the official report of the *Fiala* gives it as six minutes. And then it began to rain in torrents until he was almost drowned. A great wind arose and lashed the ocean, and a whirlpool seized the falukah and whirled it round and round. Darkness descended upon the earth, and in the general mess Mohammed hit his head a terrific blow against the mast. He was sure it was but a matter of seconds before they would be dashed to pieces by the waves. The falukah spun like a marine top with a swift sideways motion. Something was dragging them along, sucking them in. The *Fiala* went careening by, her fighting masts hanging in shreds. The air was full of falling rocks, trees, splinters, and thick clouds of dust that turned the water yellow in the lightning flashes. The mast went crashing over and a lemon tree descended to take its place. Great streams of lava poured down out of the air, and masses of opaque matter plunged into the sea all about the falukah. Scalding mud, stones, hail, fell upon the deck.

And still the fishing-boat, gyrating like a leaf, remained afloat with its crew of half-crazed Arabs. Suffocated, stunned, scalded, petrified with fear, they lay among the mullet while the falukah raced along in its wild dance with death. Mohammed recalls seeing what he thought to be a great cliff rush by close beside them. The falukah plunged over a waterfall and was almost submerged, was caught again in a maelstrom, and went twirling on in the blackness. They all were deathly sick, but were too terrified to move.

And then the nearer roaring ceased. The air was less congested. They were still showered with sand, clods of earth, twigs, and pebbles, it is true, but the genii had stopped hurling mountains at each other. The darkness became less opaque, the water smoother. Soon they could see the moon through the clouds of settling dust, and gradually they could discern the stars. The falukah was rocking gently upon a broad expanse of muddy ocean, surrounded by a yellow scum broken here and there by a floating tree. The *Fiala* had vanished. No light shone upon the face of the waters. But death had not overtaken them. Overcome by exhaustion and terror Mohammed lay among the mullet, his legs entangled in the lemon tree. Did he dream it? He cannot tell. But as he lost consciousness he thinks he saw a star shooting toward the north.

When he awoke the falukah lay motionless upon a boundless ochre sea. They were beyond sight of land. Out of a sky slightly dim the sun burned pitilessly down, sending warmth into their bodies and courage to their hearts. All about them upon the water floated the evidences of the cataclysm of the preceding night—trees, shrubs, dead birds, and the distorted corpse of a camel. Kneeling without their prayer rugs among the mullet they raised their voices in praise of Allah and his Prophet.

VII

WITHIN twenty-four hours of the destruction of the Mountains of Atlas by the Flying Ring and the consequent flooding of the Sahara, the official gazettes and such newspapers as were still published announced that the Powers had agreed upon an armistice and accepted a proposition of mediation on the part of the United States looking toward permanent peace. The news of the devastation and flood caused by this strange and terrible dreadnought of the air created the profoundest apprehension and caused the wildest rumours, for what had happened in Tunis was assumed as likely to occur in London, Paris, or New York. Wireless messages flashed the story from Algiers to Cartagena, and it was thence disseminated throughout the civilized world by the wireless stations at Paris, Nauen, Moscow, and Georgetown.

The fact that the rotation of the earth had been retarded was still a secret, and the appearance of the

Ring had not as yet been connected with any of the extraordinary phenomena surrounding it; but the newspaper editorials universally agreed that whatever nation owned and controlled this new instrument of war could dictate its own terms. It was generally supposed that the blasting of the mountain chain of Northern Africa had been an experiment to test and demonstrate the powers of this new demoniacal invention, and in view of its success it did not seem surprising that the nations had hastened to agree to an armistice, for the Power that controlled a force capable of producing such an extraordinary physical cataclysm could annihilate every capital, every army, every people upon the globe or even the globe itself.

The flight of the Ring machine had been observed at several different points, beginning at Cape Race, where at about four A. M. the wireless operator reported what he supposed to be a large comet discharging earthward a diagonal shaft of orange-yellow light and moving at incredible velocity in a southeasterly direction. During the following day the lookout on the *Vira*, a fishguard and scout cruiser of the North Atlantic Patrol, saw a black speck soaring among the clouds which he took to be a lost monoplane fighting to regain the coast of Ireland. At sundown an amateur wireless operator at St. Michael's in the Azores noted a small comet sweeping across the sky far to the north. This comet an hour or so later passed directly over the cities of Lisbon, Linares, Lorca, Cartagena, and Algiers, and was clearly observable from Badajoz, Almadén, Seville, Cordova, Grenada, Oran, Biskra, and Tunis, and at the latter places it was easily possible for telescopic observers to determine its size, shape, and general construction.

Daniel W. Quinn, Jr., the acting United States Consul stationed at Biskra, who happened to be dining with the abbot of the Franciscan monastery at Linares, sent the following account of the flight of the Ring to the State Department at Washington, where it is now on file. [See Vol. 27, pp. 491-498, with footnote, of Official Records of the Consular Correspondence for 1915-1916.] After describing general conditions in Algeria he continues:

"We had gone upon the roof in the early evening to look at the sky through the large telescope presented to the Franciscans by Count Philippe d'Ormay, when Father Antoine called my attention to a comet

THE MAN WHO ROCKED THE EARTH

that was apparently coming straight toward us. Instead, however, of leaving a horizontal trail of fire behind it, this comet or meteorite seemed to shoot an almost vertical beam of orange light toward the earth. It produced a very strange effect on all of us, since a normal comet or other celestial body that left a wake of light of that sort behind it would naturally be expected to be moving upward toward the zenith, instead of in a direction parallel to the earth. It looked somehow as if the tail of the comet had been bent over. As soon as it came near enough so that we could focus the telescope upon it we discovered that it was a new sort of flying machine. It passed over our heads at a height no greater than ten thousand feet, if as great as that, and we could see that it was a cylindrical ring like a doughnut or an anchor ring, constructed, I believe, of highly polished metal, the inner aperture being about twenty-five yards in diameter. The tube of the cylinder looked to be about twenty feet thick, and had circular windows or portholes that were brilliantly lighted.

"The strangest thing about it was that it carried a superstructure consisting of a number of arms meeting at a point above the centre of the opening and supporting some sort of apparatus from which the beam of light emanated. This appliance, which we supposed to be a gigantic searchlight, was focused down through the Ring and could apparently be moved at will over a limited radius of about fifteen degrees. We could not understand this, nor why the light was thrown from outside and above instead of from inside the flying machine, but the explanation may be found in the immense heat that must have been required to generate the light, since it illuminated the entire country for fifty miles or so, and we were able to read without trouble the fine print of the abbot's rubric. This Flying Ring moved on an even keel at the tremendous velocity of about two hundred miles an hour. We wondered what would happen if it turned turtle, for in that case the weight of the superstructure would have rendered it impossible for the machine to right itself. In fact, none of us had ever imagined any such air monster before. Beside it a Zeppelin seemed like a wooden toy.

"The Ring passed over the mountains toward Cabes and within a short time a volcanic eruption occurred that destroyed a section of the Atlas Range." [Mr. Quinn here describes with considerable detail the destruction of the mountains.] "The next morning I found Biskra crowded with Arabs, who reported that the ocean had poured through the passage made by the eruption and was flooding the entire desert as far south as the oasis of Wargla, and that it had come within twelve miles of the walls of our own city. I at once hired a donkey and made a personal investigation, with the result that I can report as a fact that the entire desert east and south of Biskra is inundated to a depth of from seven to ten feet and that the water gives no sign of going down. The loss of life seems to have been negligible, owing to the fact that the height of the water is not great and that many unexpected islands have provided safety for the caravans that were *in transitu*. These are now marooned and waiting for assistance, which I am informed will be sent from Cabes in the form of flat-bottomed boats fitted with motor auxiliaries.

"Respectfully submitted,
"D. W. QUINN, JR.,
"Acting U. S. Consul."

The Italian cruiser *Fiala*, which had been carried one hundred and eighty miles into the desert on the night of the eruption, grounded safely on the plateau of Tasili, but the volcanic tidal wave on which she had been swept along, having done its work, receded, leaving too little water for the *Fiala's* draft of thirty-seven feet. Four launches sent out in different directions to the south and east reported no sign of land, but immense quantities of floating vegetable matter, yellow dust, and the bodies of jackals, camels, zebras, and lions. The fifth launch after great hardships reached the seacoast through the new channel and arrived at Sfax after eight days.

The mean tide level of the Mediterranean sank fifteen inches, and the water showed marked discoloration for several months, while a volcanic haze hung over Northern Africa, Sicily, Malta, and Sardinia for an even longer period.

Though many persons must have lost their lives

the records are incomplete in this respect; but there is a curious document in the mosque at Sfax touching the effect of the Lavender Ray. It appears that an Arab mussel-gatherer was in a small boat with his two brothers at the time the Ring appeared above the mountains. As they looked up toward the sky the Ray flashed over and illuminated their faces. They thought nothing of it at the time, for almost immediately the mountains were rent asunder and in the titanic upheaval that followed they were all cast upon the shore, as they thought, dead men. Reaching Sfax they reported their adventures and offered prayers in gratitude for their extraordinary escape; but five days later all three began to suffer excruciating torment from internal burns, the skin upon their heads and bodies began to peel off, and they died in agony within the week.

VIII

IT WAS but a few days thereafter that the President of the United States received the official note from Count von Koenitz, on behalf of the Imperial German Commissioners, to the effect that Germany would join with the other Powers in an armistice looking toward peace and ultimately a universal disarmament. Similar notes had already been received by the President from France, Great Britain, Russia, Italy, Austria, Spain, and Slavia, and a multitude of the other smaller Powers who were engaged in the war, and there was no longer any reason for delaying the calling of an international council or diet for the purpose of bringing about what Pax demanded as a ransom for the safety of the globe.

In the files of the State Department at Washington there is secreted the only record of the diplomatic correspondence touching these momentous events, and a transcript of the messages exchanged between the President of the United States and the Arbiter of

Human Destiny. They are comparatively few in number, for Pax seemed to be satisfied to leave all details to the Powers themselves. In the interest of saving time, however, he made the simple suggestion that the present ambassadors should be given plenary powers to determine the terms and conditions upon which universal peace should be declared. All these proceedings and the reasons therefore were kept profoundly secret. It began to look as though the matter would be put through with characteristic Yankee promptness. Pax's suggestion was acceded to, and the ambassadors and ministers were given unrestricted latitude in drawing the treaty that should abolish war forever.

Now that he had been won over no one was more indefatigable than Von Koenitz, none more fertile in suggestions. It was he who drafted with his own hand the forty pages devoted to the creation of the commission charged with the duty of destroying all arms, munitions, and implements of war; and he not only acted as chairman of the preliminary drafting committee, but was an active member of at least half a dozen other important subcommittees. The President daily communicated the progress of this con-

THE MAN WHO ROCKED THE EARTH 71

ference of the Powers to Pax through Bill Hood, and received daily in return a hearty if laconic approval.

"I am satisfied of the sincerity of the Powers and with the progress made. PAX."

was the ordinary type of message received. Meantime word had been sent to all the governments that an indefinite armistice had been declared, to commence at the end of ten days, for it had been found necessary to allow for the time required to transmit the orders to the various fields of military operations throughout Europe. In the interim the war continued.

It was at this time that Count von Koenitz, who now was looked upon as the leading figure of the conference, arose and said: "Your Excellencies, this distinguished diet will, I doubt not, presently conclude its labours and receive not only the approval of the Powers represented but the gratitude of the nations of the world. I voice the sentiments of the Imperial Commissioners when I say that no Power looks forward with greater eagerness than Germany to the accomplishment of our purpose. But we should not forget that there is one menace to mankind greater than that of war—namely, the lurking danger from the power of this unknown possessor of superhuman knowledge of explosives. So far his influence has been a benign one, but who can say when it may become malignant? Will our labours please him? Perhaps not. Shall we agree? I hope so, but who can tell? Will our armies lay down their arms even after we have agreed? I believe all will go well; but is it wise for us to refrain from jointly taking steps to ascertain the identity of this unknown juggler with Nature, and the source of his power? It is my own opinion, since we cannot exert any influence or control upon this individual, that we should take whatever steps are within our grasp to safeguard ourselves in the event that he refuses to keep faith with us. To this end I suggest an international conference of scientific men from all the nations to be held here in Washington coincidently with our own meetings, with a view to determining these questions."

His remarks were greeted with approval by almost all the representatives present except Sir John Smith, who mildly hinted that such a course might be regarded as savouring a trifle of double dealing. Should Pax receive knowledge of the suggested conference he might question their sincerity and view all

THE MAN WHO ROCKED THE EARTH 73

their doings with suspicion. In a word, Sir John believed in following a consistent course and treating Pax as a friend and ally and not as a possible enemy.

Sir John's speech, however, left the delegates unconvinced and with the feeling that his argument was over-refined. They felt that there could be no objection to endeavouring to ascertain the source of Pax's power—the law of self-preservation seemed to indicate such a course as necessary. And it had, in fact, already been discussed vaguely by several less conspicuous delegates. Accordingly it was voted, with but two dissenting voices,* to summon what was known as Conference No. 2, to be held as soon as possible, its proceedings to be conducted in secret under the auspices of the National Academy of Sciences, with the president of the Academy acting as permanent chairman. To this conference the President appointed Thornton as one of the three delegates from the United States.

The council of the Powers having so voted, Count von Koenitz at once transmitted, by way of Sayville, a message which in code appeared to be addressed to

---
*The President of the United States also voted in the negative.

a Herr Karl Heinweg, Notary, at 12 ᴮᴵˢ Bunden Strasse, Strassburg, and related to a mortgage about to fall due upon some of Von Koenitz's properties in Thüringen. When decoded it read:

"*To the Imperial Commissioners of the German Federated States:*

"I have the honour to report that acting according to your distinguished instructions I have this day proposed an international conference to consider the scientific problems presented by certain recent phenomena and that my proposition was adopted. I believe that in this way the proceedings here may be delayed indefinitely and time thus secured to enable an expedition to be organized and dispatched for the purpose of destroying this unknown person or ascertaining the secret of his power, in accordance with my previous suggestion. It would be well to send as delegates to this Conference No. 2 several professors of physics who can by plausible arguments and ingenious theories so confuse the matter that no determination can be reached. I suggest Professors Gasgabelaus, of München, and Leybach, of the Hague.

"Von Koenitz."

And having thus fulfilled his duty the count took a cab to the Metropolitan Club and there played a discreet game of billiards with Señor Tomasso Varilla, the ex-minister from Argentina.

THE MAN WHO ROCKED THE EARTH 75

Von Koenitz from the first had played his hand with a skill which from a diplomatic view left nothing to be desired. The extraordinary natural phenomena which had occurred coincidentally with the first message of Pax to the President of the United States and the fall of Cleopatra's Needle had been immediately observed by the scientists attached to the Imperial and other universities throughout the German Federated States, and had no sooner been observed than their significance had been realized. These most industrious and thorough of all human investigators had instantly reported the facts and their preliminary conclusions to the Imperial Commissioners, with the recommendation that no stone be left unturned in attempting to locate and ascertain the causes of this disruption of the forces of nature. The Commissioners at once demanded an exhaustive report from the faculty of the Imperial German University, and notified Von Koenitz by cable that until further notice he must seek in every way to delay investigation by other nations and to belittle the importance of what had occurred, for these astute German scientists had at once jumped to the conclusion that the acceleration of the earth's motion had been due to some human agency possessed of a hitherto unsuspected power.

It was for this reason that at the first meeting at the White House the Ambassador had pooh-poohed the whole matter and talked of snowstorms in the Alps and showers of fish at Heidelburg, but with the rending of the northern coast of Africa and the well-attested appearances of "The Ring" he soon reached the conclusion that his wisest course was to cause such a delay on the part of the other Powers that the inevitable race for the secret would be won by the nation which he so astutely represented. He reasoned, quite accurately, that the scientists of England, Russia, and America would not remain idle in attempting to deduce the cause and place the origin of the phenomena and the habitat of the master of the Ring, and that the only effectual means to enable Germany to capture this, the greatest of all prizes of war, was to befuddle the representatives of the other nations while leaving his own unhampered in their efforts to accomplish that which would make his countrymen, almost without further effort, the masters of the world. Now the easiest way to befuddle the scientists of the world was to get them into one place and befuddle them all together, and this, after communicating with his superiors, he had proceeded to do. He was a clever man, trained in the devious ways of the Wilhelmstrasse, and when he set out to accomplish something he was almost inevitably successful. Yet in spite of the supposed alliance between Kaiser and Deity man proposes and God disposes, and sometimes the latter uses the humblest of human instruments in that disposition.

IX

THE Imperial German Commissioner for War, General Hans von Helmuth, was a man of extraordinary decision and farsightedness. Sixty years of age, he had been a member of the general staff since he was forty. He had sat at the feet of Bismarck and Von Moltke, and during his active participation in the management of German military affairs he had seen but slight changes in their policy: Mass—overwhelming mass; sudden momentous onslaught, and, above all, an attack so quick that your adversary could not regain his feet. It worked nine times out of ten, and when it didn't it was usually better than taking the defensive. General von Helmuth having an approved system was to that extent relieved of anxiety, for all he had to do was to work out details. In this his highly efficient organization was almost automatic. He himself was a human compendium of knowledge, and he had but to press a button and emit a few gutturals and any information that he wanted lay typewritten before him. Now he sat in his office smoking a Bremen cigar and studying a huge Mercatorial projection of the Atlantic and adjacent countries, while with the fingers of his left hand he combed his heavy beard.

From the window he looked down upon the inner fortifications of Mainz—to which city the capital had been removed three months before—and upon the landing stage for the scouting planes which were constantly arriving or whirring off toward Holland or Strassburg. Across the river, under the concealed guns of a sunken battery, stood the huge hangars of the now useless dirigibles Z^{51-57}. The landing stage communicated directly by telephone with the adjutant's office, an enormous hall filled with maps, with which Von Helmuth's private room was connected. The adjutant himself, a worried-looking man with a bullet head and an iron-gray moustache, stood at a table in the centre of the hall addressing rapid-fire sentences to various persons who appeared in the doorway, saluted, and hurried off again. Several groups were gathered about the table and the adjutant carried on an interrupted conversation with all of them, pausing to read the telegrams and messages that shot out of the pneumatic tubes upon the table from the telegraph and telephone office on the floor below.

An elderly man in rather shabby clothes entered, looking about helplessly through the thick lenses of his double spectacles, and the adjutant turned at once from the officers about him with an "Excuse me, gentlemen."

"Good afternoon, Professor von Schwenitz; the general is waiting for you," said he. "This way, please."

He stalked across to the door of the inner office.

"Professor von Schwenitz is here," he announced, and immediately returned to take up the thread of his conversation in the centre of the hall.

The general turned gruffly to greet his visitor. "I have sent for you, Professor," said he, without removing his cigar, "in order that I may fully understand the method by which you say you have ascertained the place of origin of the wireless messages and electrical disturbances referred to in our communications of last week. This may be a serious matter.

The accuracy of your information is of vital importance."

The professor hesitated in embarrassment, and the general scowled.

"Well?" he demanded, biting off the chewed end of his cigar. "Well? This is not a lecture room. Time is short. Out with it."

"Your Excellency!" stammered the poor professor, "I—I—— The observations are so—inadequate—one cannot determine——"

"What?" roared Von Helmuth. "But you said you *had!*"

"Only approximately, your Excellency. One cannot be positive, but within a reasonable distance ——" He paused.

"What do you call a reasonable distance? I supposed your physics was an exact science!" retorted the general.

"But the data——"

"What do you call a reasonable distance?" bellowed the Imperial Commissioner.

"A hundred kilometres!" suddenly shouted the overwrought professor, losing control of himself. "I won't be talked to this way, do you hear? I won't!

How can a man think? I'm a member of the faculty of the Imperial University. I've been decorated twice—twice!"

"Fiddlesticks!" returned the general, amused in spite of himself. "Don't be absurd. I merely wish you to hurry. Have a cigar?"

"Oh, your Excellency!" protested the professor, now both ashamed and frightened. "You must excuse me. The war has shattered my nerves. May I smoke? Thank you."

"Sit down. Take your time," said Von Helmuth, looking out and up at a monoplane descending toward the landing in slowly lessening spirals.

"You see, your Excellency," explained Von Schwenitz, "the data are fragmentary, but I used three methods, each checking the others."

"The first?" shot back the general. The monoplane had landed safely.

"I compared the records of all the seimographs that had registered the earthquake wave attendant on the electrical discharges accompanying the great yellow auroras of July. These shocks had been felt all over the globe, and I secured reports from Java, New Guinea, Lima, Tucson, Greenwich, Algeria,

THE MAN WHO ROCKED THE EARTH 83

and Moscow. These showed the wave had originated somewhere in Eastern Labrador."

"Yes, yes. Go on!" ordered the general.

"In the second place, the violent magnetic storms produced by the helium aurora appear to have left their mark each time upon the earth in a permanent, if slight, deflection of the compass needle. The earth's normal magnetic field seems to have had superimposed upon it a new field comprised of lines of force nearly parallel to the equator. My computations show that these great circles of magnetism centre at approximately the same point in Labrador as that indicated by the seismographs—about fifty-five degrees north and seventy-five degrees west."

The general seemed struck with this.

"Permanent deflection, you say!" he ejaculated.

"Yes, apparently permanent. Finally the barometer records told the same story, although in less precise form. A compressional wave of air had been started in the far north and had spread out over the earth with the velocity of sound. Though the barographs themselves gave no indication whence this wave had come, the variation in its intensity at different meteorological observatories could be accounted for by the law of inverse squares on the supposition that the explosion which started the wave had occurred at fifty-five degrees north, seventy-five degrees west."

The professor paused and wiped his glasses. With a roar a Taube slid off the landing stage, shot over toward the hangars, and soared upward.

"Is that all?" inquired the general, turning again to the chart.

"That is all, your Excellency," answered Von Schwenitz.

"Then you may go!" muttered the Imperial Commissioner. "If we find the source of these disturbances where you predict you will receive the Black Eagle."

"Oh, your Excellency!" protested the professor, his face shining with satisfaction.

"And if we do *not* find it—there will be a vacancy on the faculty of the Imperial University!" he added grimly. "Good afternoon."

He pressed a button and the departing scholar was met by an orderly and escorted from the War Bureau, while the adjutant joined Von Helmuth.

"He's got him! I'm satisfied!" remarked the Commissioner. "Now outline your plan."

The bullet-headed man took up the calipers and indicated a spot on the coast of Labrador:

"Our expedition will land, subject to your approval, at Hamilton Inlet, using the town of Rigolet as a base. By availing ourselves of the Nascopee River and the lakes through which it flows, we can easily penetrate to the highland where the inventor of the Ring machine has located himself. The auxiliary brigantine *Sea Fox* is lying now under American colours at Amsterdam, and as she can steam fifteen knots an hour she should reach the Inlet in about ten days, passing to the north of the Orkneys."

"What force have you in mind?" inquired Von Helmuth, his cold gray eyes narrowing.

"Three full companies of sappers and miners, ten mountain howitzers, a field battery, fifty rapid-fire standing rifles, and a complete outfit for throwing lyddite. Of course we shall rely principally on high explosives if it becomes necessary to use force, but what we want is a hostage who may later become an ally."

"Yes, of course," said the general with a laugh. "This is a scientific, not a military, expedition."

"I have asked Lieutenant Münster to report upon the necessary equipment."

Von Helmuth nodded, and the adjutant stepped to the door and called out: "Lieutenant Münster!"

A trim young man in naval uniform appeared upon the threshold and saluted.

"State what you regard as necessary as equipment for the proposed expedition," said the general.

"Twenty motor boats, each capable of towing several flat-bottomed barges or native canoes, forty mules, a field telegraph, and also a high-powered wireless apparatus, axes, spades, wire cables and drums, windlasses, dynamite for blasting, and provisions for sixty days. We shall live off the country and secure artisans and bearers from among the natives."

"When will it be possible to start?" inquired the general.

"In twelve days if you give the order now," answered the young man.

"Very well, you may go. And good luck to you!" he added.

THE MAN WHO ROCKED THE EARTH 87

The young lieutenant saluted and turned abruptly on his heel.

Over the parade ground a biplane was hovering, darting this way and that, rising and falling with startling velocity.

"Who's that?" inquired the general approvingly.

"Schöningen," answered the adjutant.

The Imperial Commissioner felt in his breast-pocket for another cigar.

"Do you know, Ludwig," he remarked amiably as he struck a meditative match, "sometimes I more than half believe this 'Flying Ring' business is all rot!"

The adjutant looked pained.

"And yet," continued Von Helmuth, "if Bismarck could see one of those things," he waved his cigar toward the gyrating aeroplane, "he wouldn't believe it."

X

ALL day the International Assembly of Scientists, officially known as Conference No. 2, had been sitting, but not progressing, in the large lecture hall of the Smithsonian Institution, which probably had never before seen so motley a gathering. Each nation had sent three representatives, two professional scientists, and a lay delegate, the latter some writer or thinker renowned in his own country for his wide knowledge and powers of ratiocination. They had come together upon the appointed day, although the delegates from the remoter countries had not yet arrived, and the Committee on Credentials had already reported. Germany had sent Gasgabelaus, Leybach, and Wilhelm Lamszus; France—Sortell, Amand, and Buona Varilla; Great Britain—Sir William Crookes, Sir Francis Soddy, and Mr. H. G. Wells, celebrated for his "The War of the Worlds" and The "World Set Free," and hence supposedly just the man to unravel a scientific mystery such as that which confronted this galaxy of immortals.

The Committee on Data, of which Thornton was a member, having been actively at work for nearly two weeks through wireless communication with all the observatories—seismatic, meteorological, astronomical, and otherwise—throughout the world, had reduced its findings to print, and this matter, translated into French, German, and Italian, had already been distributed among those present. Included in its pages was Quinn's letter to the State Department.

The roll having been called, the president of the National Academy of Sciences made a short speech in which he outlined briefly the purpose for which the committee had been summoned and commented to some extent upon the character of the phenomena it was required to analyze.

And then began an unending series of discussions and explanations in French, German, Dutch, Russian, and Italian, by goggle-eyed, bushy-whiskered, long-haired men who looked like anarchists or sociologists and apparently had never before had an unrestricted opportunity to air their views on anything.

Thornton, listening to this hodgepodge of technicalities, was dismayed and distrustful. These men spoke a language evidently familiar to them, which he, although a professional scientist, found a meaningless jargon. The whole thing seemed unreal, had a purely theoretic or literary quality about it that made him question even their premises. In the tainted air of the council room, listening to these little potbellied *Professoren* from Amsterdam and München, doubt assailed him, doubt even that the earth had changed its orbit, doubt even of his own established formulæ and tables. Weren't they all just talking through their hats? Wasn't it merely a game in which an elaborate system of equivalents gave a semblance of actuality to what in fact was nothing but mind-play? Even Wells, whose literary style he admired as one of the beauties as well as one of the wonders of the world, had been a disappointment. He had seemed singularly halting and unconvincing.

"I wish I knew a practical man—I wish Bennie Hooker were here!" muttered Thornton to himself. He had not seen his classmate Hooker for twenty-six years; but that was one thing about Hooker: you knew he'd be exactly the same—only more so—as he was when you last saw him. In those years Bennie had become the Lawson Professor of Applied Physics at Harvard. Thornton had read his papers on induced radiation, thermic equilibrium, and had one of Bennie's famous Gem Home Cookers in his own little bachelor apartment. Hooker would know. And if he didn't he'd tell you so, without befogging the atmosphere with a lot of things he *did* know, but that wouldn't help you in the least. Thornton clutched at the thought of him like a falling aeronaut at a dangling rope. He'd be worth a thousand of these dreaming lecturers, these beer-drinking visionaries! But where could he be found? It was August, vacation time. Still, he might be in Cambridge giving a summer course or something.

At that moment Professor Gasgabelaus, the temporary chairman, a huge man, the periphery of whose abdomen rivalled the circumference of the "working terrestrial globe" at the other end of the platform, pounded perspiringly with his gavel and announced that the conference would adjourn until the following Monday morning. It was Friday afternoon, so he had sixty hours in which to connect with Bennie, if Bennie could be discovered. A telegram of inquiry brought no response, and he took the midnight train to Boston, reaching Cambridge about two o'clock the following afternoon.

The air trembled with heat. Only by dodging from the shadow of one big elm to another did he manage to reach the Appian Way—the street given in the university catalogue as Bennie's habitat—alive. As he swung open the little wicket gate he realized with an odd feeling that it was the same house where Hooker had lived when a student, twenty-five years before.

"Board" was printed on a yellow, fly-blown card in the corner of the window beside the door.

Up there over the porch was the room Bennie had inhabited from '85 to '89. He recalled vividly the night he, Thornton, had put his foot through the lower pane. They had filled up the hole with an old golf stocking. His eyes searched curiously for the pane. There it was, still broken and still stuffed—it couldn't be!—with some colourless material strangely resembling disintegrating worsted. The sun smote him in the back of his neck and drove him to seek the relief of the porch. Had he ever left Cambridge? Wasn't it a dream about his becoming an astronomer and working at the Naval Observatory? And all this stuff about the earth going on the loose? If he opened the door wouldn't he find Bennie with a towel round his head cramming for the "exams"? For a moment he really imagined that he was an undergraduate. Then as he fanned himself with his straw hat he caught, on the silk band across the interior, the words: "Smith's Famous Headwear, Washington, D. C." No, he was really an astronomer.

He shuddered in spite of the heat as he pulled the bell knob. What ghosts would its jangle summon? The bell, however, gave no sound; in fact the knob came off in his hand, followed by a foot or so of copper wire. He laughed, gazing at it blankly. No one had ever used the bell in the old days. They had simply kicked open the door and halloed: "O-o-h, Bennie Hooker!"

Thornton laid the knob on the piazza and inspected the front of the house. The windows were thick with dust, the "yard" scraggly with weeds. A piece of string held the latch of the gate together. Then automatically, and without intending to do so at all, Thornton turned the handle of the front door, assisting it coincidentally with a gentle kick from his right toe, and found himself in the narrow cabbage-scented hallway. The old, familiar, battered black-walnut hatrack of his student days leaned drunkenly against the wall—Thornton knew one of its back legs was missing—and on the imitation marble slab was a telegram addressed to "Professor Benjamin Hooker." And also, instinctively, Thornton lifted up his adult voice and yelled:

"O-o-h, ye-ay! Bennie Hooker!"

The volume of his own sound startled him. Instantly he saw the ridiculousness of it—he, the senior astronomer at the Naval Observatory, yelling like that——

"O-o-h, ye-ay!" came in smothered tones from above.

Thornton bounded up the stairs, two, three steps at a time, and pounded on the old door over the porch.

"Go away!" came back the voice of Bennie Hooker. "Don't want any lunch!"

Thornton continued to bang on the door while Professor Hooker wrathfully besought the intruder to depart before he took active measures. There was the cracking of glass.

"Oh, damn!" came from inside.

Thornton rattled the knob and kicked. Somebody haltingly crossed the room, the key turned, and Prof. Bennie Hooker opened the door.

"Well?" he demanded, scowling over his thick spectacles.

"Hello, Bennie!" said Thornton, holding out his hand.

"Hello, Buck!" returned Hooker. "Come in. I thought it was that confounded Ethiopian."

As far as Thornton could see, it was the same old room, only now crammed with books and pamphlets and crowded with tables of instruments. Hooker, clad in sneakers, white ducks, and an undershirt, was smoking a small "T. D." pipe.

"Where on earth did you come from?" he inquired good-naturedly.

"Washington," answered Thornton, and something told him that this was the real thing—the "goods"—that his journey would be repaid.

Hooker waved the "T. D." in a general sort of way toward some broken-down horsehair armchairs and an empty crate.

"Sit down, won't you?" he said, as if he had seen

his guest only the day before. He looked vaguely about for something that Thornton might smoke, then seated himself on a cluttered bench holding a number of retorts, beside which flamed an oxyacetylene blowpipe. He was a wizened little chap, with scrawny neck and protruding Adam's apple. His long hair gave no evidence of the use of the comb, and his hands were the hands of Esau. He had an alertness that suggested a robin, but at the same time gave the impression that he looked through things rather than at them. On the mantel was a saucer containing the fast oxidizing cores of several apples and a half-eaten box of oatmeal biscuits.

"My Lord! This is an untidy hole! No more order than when you were an undergrad!" exclaimed Thornton, looking about him in amused horror.

"Order?" returned Bennie indignantly. "Everything's in perfect order! This chair is filled with the letters I *have* already answered; this chair with the letters I've *not* answered; and this chair with the letters I shall *never* answer!"

Thornton took a seat on the crate, laughing. It was the same old Bennie!

"You're an incorrigible!" he sighed despairingly.

"Well, you're a star gazer, aren't you?" inquired Hooker, relighting his pipe. "Some one told me so—I forget who. You must have a lot of interesting problems. They tell me that new planet of yours is full of uranium."

Thornton laughed. "You mustn't believe all that you read in the papers. What are you working at particularly?"

"Oh, radium and thermic induction mostly," answered Hooker. "And when I want a rest I take a crack at the fourth dimension—spacial curvature's my hobby. But I'm always working at radio stuff. That's where the big things are going to be pulled off, you know."

"Yes, of course," answered Thornton. He wondered if Hooker ever saw a paper, how long since he had been out of the house. "By the way, did you know Berlin had been taken?" he asked.

"Berlin—in Germany, you mean?"

"Yes, by the Russians."

"No! Has it?" inquired Hooker with politeness. "Oh, I think some one did mention it."

Thornton fumbled for a cigarette and Bennie handed him a match. They seemed to have extraordinarily little to say for men who hadn't seen each other for twenty-six years.

"I suppose," went on the astronomer, "you think it's deuced funny my dropping in casually this way after all this time, but the fact is I came on purpose. I want to get some information from you straight."

"Go ahead!" said Bennie. "What's it about?"

"Well, in a word," answered Thornton, "the earth's nearly a quarter of an hour behind time."

Hooker received this announcement with a polite interest but no astonishment.

"That's a how-de-do!" he remarked. "What's done it?"

"That's what I want you to tell *me*," said Thornton sternly. "What *could* do it?"

Hooker unlaced his legs and strolled over to the mantel.

"Have a cracker?" he asked, helping himself. Then he picked up a piece of wood and began whittling. "I suppose there's the devil to pay?" he suggested. "Things upset and so on? Atmospheric changes? When did it happen?"

"About three weeks ago. Then there's this Sahara business."

"What Sahara business?"

"Haven't you heard?"

"No," answered Hooker rather impatiently. "I haven't heard anything. I haven't any time to read the papers; I'm too busy. My thermic inductor transformers melted last week and I'm all in the air. What was it?"

"Oh, never mind now," said Thornton hurriedly, perceiving that Hooker's ignorance was an added asset. He'd get his science pure, uncontaminated by disturbing questions of fact. "How about the earth's losing that quarter of an hour?"

"Of course she's off her orbit," remarked Hooker in a detached way. "And you want to know what's done it? Don't blame you. I suppose you've gone into the possibilities of stellar attraction."

"Discount that!" ordered Thornton. "What I want to know is whether it could happen from the inside?"

"Why not?" inquired Hooker. "A general shift in the mass would do it. So would the mere application of force at the proper point."

"It never happened before."

"Of course not. Neither had seedless oranges until Burbank came along," said Hooker.

"Do you regard it as possible by any human agency?" inquired Thornton.

"Why not?" repeated Hooker. "All you need is the energy. And it's lying all round if you could only get at it. That's just what I'm working at now. Radium, uranium, thorium, actinium—all the radio-active elements—are, as everybody knows, continually disintegrating, discharging the enormous energy that is imprisoned in their molecules. It may take generations, epochs, centuries, for them to get rid of it and transform themselves into other substances, but they will inevitably do so eventually. They're doing with more or less of a rush what all the elements are doing at their leisure. A single ounce of uranium contains about the same amount of energy that could be produced by the combustion of ten tons of coal—but it won't let the energy go. Instead it holds on to it, and the energy leaks slowly, almost imperceptibly, away, like water from a big reservoir tapped only by a tiny pipe. 'Atomic energy' Rutherford calls it. Every element, every substance, has its ready to be touched off and put to use. The chap who can find out how to release that energy all at once will revolutionize the civilized world. It will be like the discovery that water could be turned into steam and made to work for us—multiplied a million times. If, instead of that energy just oozing away and the uranium disintegrating infinitesimally each year, it could be exploded at a given moment you could drive an ocean liner with a handful of it. You could make the old globe stagger round and turn upside down! Mankind could just lay off and take a holiday. But *how?*"

Bennie enthusiastically waved his pipe at Thornton.

"How! That's the question. Everybody's known about the possibilities, for Soddy wrote a book about it; but nobody's ever suggested where the key could be found to unlock that treasure-house of energy. Some chap made up a novel once and pretended it was done, but he didn't say *how*. "But —and he lowered his voice passionately—"I'm working at it, and—and—I've nearly—nearly got it."

Thornton, infected by his friend's excitement, leaned forward in his chair.

"Yes—nearly. If only my transformers hadn't melted! You see I got the idea from Savaroff, who noticed that the activity of radium and other elements wasn't constant, but varied with the degree of solar activity, reaching its maximum at the periods when the sun spots were most numerous. In other words, he's shown that the breakdown of the atoms of radium and the other radioactive elements isn't spontaneous, as Soddy and others had thought, but is due to the action of certain extremely penetrating rays given out by the sun. These particular rays are the result of the enormous temperature of the solar atmosphere, and their effect upon radioactive substances is analogous to that of the detonating cap upon dynamite. No one has been able to produce these rays in the laboratory, although Hempel has suspected sometimes that traces of them appeared in the radiations from powerful electric sparks. Everything came to a halt until Hiroshito discovered thermic induction, and we were able to elevate temperature almost indefinitely through a process similar to the induction of high electric potentials by means of transformers and the Ruhmkorff coil.

"Hiroshito wasn't looking for a detonating ray

and didn't have time to bother with it, but I started a series of experiments with that end in view. I got close—I am close, but the trouble has been to control the forces set in motion, for the rapid rise in temperature has always destroyed the apparatus."

Thornton whistled. "And when you succeed?" he asked in a whisper.

Hooker's face was transfigured.

"When I succeed I shall control the world," he cried, and his voice trembled. "But the damn thing either melts or explodes," he added with a tinge of indignation.

"You know about Hiroshito's experiments, of course; he used a quartz bulb containing a mixture of neon gas and the vapour of mercury, placed at the centre of a coil of silver wire carrying a big oscillatory current. This induced a ring discharge in the bulb, and the temperature of the vapour mixture rose until the bulb melted. He calculated that the temperature of that part of the vapour which carried the current was over 6,000°. You see, the ring discharge is not in contact with the wall of the bulb, and can consequently be much hotter. It's like this." Here Bennie drew with a burnt match on the back of an envelope a diagram of something which resembled a doughnut in a chianti flask.

Thornton scratched his head. "Yes," he said, "but that's an old principle, isn't it? Why does Hiro—what's his name—call it—thermic induction?"

"Oriental imagination, probably," replied Bennie. "Hiroshito observed that a sudden increase in the temperature of the discharge occurred at the moment when the silver coil of his transformer became white hot, which he explained by some mysterious inductive action of the heat vibrations. I don't follow him at all. His theory's probably all wrong, but he delivered the goods. He gave me the right tip, even if I have got him lashed to the mast now. I use a tungsten spiral in a nitrogen atmosphere in my transformer and replace the quartz bulb with a capsule of zircorundum."

"A capsule of what?" asked Thornton, whose chemistry was mid-Victorian.

"Zircorundum," said Bennie, groping around in a drawer of his work table. "It's an absolute nonconductor of heat. Look here, just stick your finger in that." He held out to Thornton what appeared to be a small test tube of black glass. Thornton, with a slight moral hesitation, did as he was told, and Bennie, whistling, picked up the oxyacetylene blowpipe, regarding it somewhat as a dog fancier might gaze at an exceptionally fine pup. "Hold up your finger," said he to the astronomer. "That's right—like that!"

Thrusting the blowpipe forward, he allowed the hissing blue-white flame to wrap itself round the outer wall of the tube—a flame which Thornton knew could melt its way through a block of steel—but the astronomer felt no sensation of heat, although he not unnaturally expected the member to be incinerated.

"Queer, eh?" said Bennie. "Absolute insulation! Beats the thermos bottle, and requires no vacuum. It isn't quite what I want though, because the disintegrating rays which the ring discharge gives out break down the zirconium, which isn't an end-product of radioactivity. The pressure in the capsule rises, due to the liberation of helium, and it blows up, and the landlady or the police come up and bother me."

Thornton was scrutinizing Bennie's rough diagram. "This ring discharge," he meditated; "I wonder if it isn't something like a sunspot. You know the spots are electron vortices with strong magnetic fields. I'll bet you the Savaroff disintegrating rays come from the spots and not from the whole surface of the sun!"

"My word," said Bennie, with a grin of delight, "you occasionally have an illuminating idea, even if you are a musty astronomer. I always thought you were a sort of calculating machine, who slept on a logarithm table. I owe you two drinks for that suggestion, and to scare a thirst into you I'll show you an experiment that no living human being has ever seen before. I can't make very powerful disintegrating rays yet, but I can break down uranium, which is the easiest of all. Later on I'll be able to disintegrate anything, if I have luck—that is, anything except end-products. Then you'll see things fly. But, for the present, just this." He picked up a thin plate of white metal. "This is the metal we're going to attack, uranium—the parent of radium—and the whole radioactive series, ending with the end-product lead."

He hung the plate by two fine wires fastened to its corners, and adjusted a coil of wire opposite its centre, while within the coil he slipped a small black capsule.

"This is the best we can do now," he said. "The capsule is made of zircorundum, and we shall get only a trace of the disintegrating rays before it blows up. But you'll see 'em, or, rather, you'll see the lavender phosphorescence of the air through which they pass."

He arranged a thick slab of plate glass between Thornton and the thermic transformer, and stepping to the wall closed a switch. An oscillatory spark discharge started off with a roar in a closed box, and the coil of wire became white hot.

"Watch the plate!" shouted Bennie.

And Thornton watched.

For ten or fifteen seconds nothing happened, and then a faint beam of pale lavender light shot out from the capsule, and the metal plate swung away from the incandescent coil as if blown by a gentle breeze.

Almost instantly there was a loud report and a blinding flash of yellow light so brilliant that for the next instant or two to Thornton's eyes the room seemed dark. Slowly the afternoon light regained its normal quality. Bennie relit his pipe unconcernedly.

"That's the germ of the idea," he said between puffs. "That capsule contains a mixture of vapours that give out disintegrating rays when the temperature is raised by thermic induction above six thousand. Most of 'em are stopped by the zirconium atoms in the capsule, which break down and liberate helium; and the temperature rises in the capsule until it explodes, as you saw just now, with a flash of yellow helium light. The rays that get out strike the uranium plate and cause the surface layer of molecules to disintegrate, their products being driven off by the atomic explosions with a velocity about equal to that of light, and it's the recoil that deflects and swings the plate. The amount of uranium decomposed in this experiment couldn't be detected by the most delicate balance—small mass, but enormous velocity. See?"

"Yes, I understand," answered Thornton. "It's the old, 'momentum equals mass times velocity,' business we had in mechanics."

"Of course this is only a toy experiment," Bennie continued. "It is what the dancing pithballs of Franklin's time were to the multipolar, high-frequency dynamo. But if we could control this force and

THE MAN WHO ROCKED THE EARTH

handle it on a large scale we could do anything with it—destroy the world, drive a car against gravity off into space, shift the axis of the earth perhaps!"

It came to Thornton as he sat there, cigarette in hand, that poor Bennie Hooker was going to receive the disappointment of his life. Within the next five minutes his dreams would be dashed to earth, for he would learn that another had stepped down to the pool of discovery before him. For how many years, he wondered, had Bennie toiled to produce his mysterious ray that should break down the atom and release the store of energy that the genii of Nature had concealed there. And now Thornton must tell him that all his efforts had gone for nothing!

"And you believe that any one who could generate a ray such as you describe could control the motion of the earth?" he asked.

"Of course, certainly," answered Hooker. "He could either disintegrate such huge quantities of matter that the mass of the earth would be shifted and its polar axis be changed, or if radioactive substances—pitchblende, for example—lay exposed upon the earth's surface he could cause them to discharge their helium and other products at such an enormous velocity that the recoil or reaction would accelerate or retard the motion of the globe. It would be quite feasible, quite simple—all one would need would be the disintegrating ray."

And then Thornton told Hooker of the flight of the giant Ring machine from the north and the destruction of the Mountains of Atlas through the apparent instrumentality of a ray of lavender light. Hooker's face turned slightly pale and his unshaven mouth tightened. Then a smile of exaltation illuminated his features.

"He's done it!" he cried joyously. "He's done it on an engineering scale. We pure-science dreamers turn up our noses at the engineers, but I tell you the improvements in the apparatus part of the game come when there is a big commercial demand for a thing and the engineering chaps take hold of it. But *who* is he and *where* is he? I must get to him. I don't suppose I can teach him much, but I've got a magnificent experiment that we can try together."

He turned to a littered writing-table and poked among the papers that lay there.

"You see," he explained excitedly, "if there is anything in the quantum theory—— Oh! but you don't care about that. The point is where *is* the chap?"

And so Thornton had to begin at the beginning and tell Hooker all about the mysterious messages and the phenomena that accompanied them. He enlarged upon Pax's benignant intentions and the great problems presented by the proposed interference of the United States Government in Continental affairs, but Bennie swept them aside. The great thing, to his mind, was to find and get into communication with Pax.

"Ah! How he must feel! The greatest achievement of all time!" cried Hooker radiantly. "How ecstatically happy! Earth blossoming like the rose! Well-watered valleys where deserts were before. War abolished, poverty, disease! Who can it be? Curie? No; she's bottled in Paris. Posky, Langham, Varanelli—it can't be any one of those fellows. It beats me! Some Hindoo or Jap maybe, but never Hiroshito! Now we must get to him right away. So much to talk over." He walked round the room, blundering into things, dizzy with the thought that his great dream had come true. Suddenly he swept everything off the table on to the floor and kicked his heels in the air.

"Hooray!" he shouted, dancing round the room like a freshman. "Hooray! Now I can take a holiday. And come to think of it, I'm as hungry as a brontosaurus!"

That night Thornton returned to Washington and was at the White House by nine o'clock the following day.

"It's all straight," he told the President. "The honestest man in the United States has said so."

XI

THE moon rose over sleeping Paris, silvering the silent reaches of the Seine, flooding the deserted streets with mellow light, yet gently retouching all the disfigurements of the siege. No lights illuminated the cafés, no taxis dashed along the boulevards, no crowds loitered in the Place de l'Opéra or the Place Vendôme. Yet save for these facts it might have been the Paris of old time, unvisited by hunger, misery, or death. The curfew had sounded. Every citizen had long since gone within, extinguished his lights, and locked his door. Safe in the knowledge that the Germans' second advance had been finally met and effectually blocked sixty miles outside the walls, and that an armistice had been declared to go into effect at midnight, Paris slumbered peacefully.

Beyond the pellet-strewn fields and glacis of the second line of defence the invader, after a series of terrific onslaughts, had paused, retreated a few miles and intrenched himself, there to wait until the starving city should capitulate. For four months he had waited, yet Paris gave no sign of surrendering. On the contrary, it seemed to have some mysterious means of self-support, and the war office, in daily communication with London, reported that it could withstand the investment for an indefinite period. Meantime the Germans reintrenched themselves, built forts of their own upon which they mounted the siege guns intended for the walls, and constructed an impregnable line of entanglements, redoubts, and defences, which rendered it impossible for any army outside the city to come to its relief.

So rose the moon, turning white the millions of slate roofs, gilding the traceries of the towers of Notre Dame, dimming the searchlights which, like the antennæ of gigantic fireflies, constantly played round the city from the summit of the Eiffel Tower. So slept Paris, confident that no crash of descending bombs would shatter the blue vault of the starlit sky or rend the habitations in which lay two millions of human beings, assured that the sun would rise through the gray mists of the Seine upon the ancient beauties of the Tuilleries and the Louvre unmarred by the enemy's projectiles, and that its citizens could pass freely along its boulevards without menace of death from flying missiles. For no shell could be hurled a distance of sixty miles, and an armistice had been declared.

Behind a small hill within the German fortifications a group of officers stood in the moonlight, examining what looked superficially like the hangar of a small dirigible. Nestling behind the hill it cast a black rectangular shadow upon the trampled sand of the redoubt. A score of artisans were busy filling a deep trench through which a huge pipe led off somewhere—a sort of deadly plumbing, for the house sheltered a monster cannon reënforced by jackets of lead and steel, the whole encased in a cooling apparatus of intricate manufacture. From the open end of the house the cylindrical barrel of the gigantic engine of war raised itself into the air at an angle of forty degrees, and from the muzzle to the ground below it was a drop of over eighty feet. On a track running off to the north rested the projectiles side by side, resembling in the dim light a row of steam boilers in the yard of a locomotive factory.

"Well," remarked one of the officers, turning to

the only one of his companions not in uniform, "'Thanatos' is ready."

The man addressed was Von Heckmann, the most famous inventor of military ordnance in the world, already four times decorated for his services to the Emperor.

"The labour of nine years!" he answered with emotion. "Nine long years of self-denial and unremitting study! But to-night I shall be repaid, repaid a thousand times."

The officers shook hands with him one after the other, and the group broke up; the men who were filling the trench completed their labours and departed; and Von Heckmann and the major-general of artillery alone remained, except for the sentries beside the gun. The night was balmy and the moon rode in a cloudless sky high above the hill. They crossed the enclosure, followed by the two sentinels, and entering a passage reached the outer wall of the redoubt, which was in turn closed and locked. Here the sentries remained, but Von Heckmann and the general continued on behind the fortifications for some distance.

"Well, shall we start the ball?" asked the general,

laying his hand on Von Heckmann's shoulder. But the inventor found it so hard to master his emotion that he could only nod his head. Yet the ball to which the general alluded was the discharging of a fiendish war machine toward an unsuspecting and harmless city alive with sleeping people, and the emotion of the inventor was due to the fact that he had devised and completed the most atrocious engine of death ever conceived by the mind of man—the Relay Gun. Horrible as is the thought, this otherwise normal man had devoted nine whole years to the problem of how to destroy human life at a distance of a hundred kilometres, and at last he had been successful, and an emperor had placed with his own divinely appointed hands a ribbon over the spot beneath which his heart should have been.

The projectile of this diabolical invention was ninty-five centimetres in diameter, and was itself a rifled mortar, which in full flight, twenty miles from the gun and at the top of its trajectory, exploded in mid-air, hurling forward its contained projectile with an additional velocity of three thousand feet per second. This process repeated itself, the final or core bomb, weighing over three hundred pounds and filled with lyddite, reaching its mark one minute and thirty-five seconds after the firing of the gun. This crowning example of the human mind's destructive ingenuity had cost the German Government five million marks and had required three years for its construction, and by no means the least of its devilish capacities was that of automatically reloading and firing itself at the interval of every ten seconds, its muzzle rising, falling, or veering slightly from side to side with each discharge, thus causing the shells to fall at wide distances. The poisonous nature of the immense volumes of gas poured out by the mastodon when in action necessitated the withdrawal of its crew to a safe distance. But once set in motion it needed no attendant. It had been tested by a preliminary shot the day before, which had been directed to a point several miles outside the walls of Paris, the effect of which had been observed and reported by high-flying German aeroplanes equipped with wireless. Everything was ready for the holocaust.

Von Heckmann and the general of artillery continued to make their way through the intrenchments and other fortifications, until at a distance of about a quarter of a mile from the redoubt where they had left the Relay Gun they arrived at a small whitewashed cottage.

"I have invited a few of my staff to join us," said the general to the inventor, "in order that they may in years to come describe to their children and their grandchildren this, the most momentous occasion in the history of warfare."

They turned the corner of the cottage and came upon a group of officers standing by the wooden gate of the cottage, all of whom saluted at their approach.

"Good evening, gentlemen," said the general. "I beg to present the members of my staff," turning to Von Heckmann.

The officers stood back while the general led the way into the cottage, the lower floor of which consisted of but a single room, used by the recent tenants as a kitchen, dining-room, and living-room. At one end of a long table, constructed by the regimental carpenter, supper had been laid, and a tub filled with ice contained a dozen or more quarts of champagne. Two orderlies stood behind the table, at the other end of which was affixed a small brass switch connected with the redoubt and controlled by a spring and button. The windows of the cottage were open, and through them poured the light of the full moon, dimming the flickering light of the candles upon the table.

In spite of the champagne, the supper, and the boxes of cigars and cigarettes, an atmosphere of solemnity was distinctly perceptible. It was as if each one of these officers, hardened to human suffering by a lifetime of discipline and active service, to say nothing of the years of horror through which they had just passed, could not but feel that in the last analysis the hurling upon an unsuspecting city of a rain of projectiles containing the highest explosive known to warfare, at a distance three times greater than that heretofore supposed to be possible to science, and the ensuing annihilation of its inhabitants, was something less for congratulation and applause than for sorrow and regret. The officers, who had joked each other outside the gate, became singularly quiet as they entered the cottage and gathered round the table where Von Heckmann and the general had taken their stand by the instrument. Utter silence fell upon the group. The mercury of their spirits dropped from summer heat to below freezing. What was this thing which they were about to do?

Through the windows, at a distance of four hundred yards, the pounding of the machinery which flooded the water jacket of the Relay Gun was distinctly audible in the stillness of the night. The pressure of a finger—a little finger—upon that electric button was all that was necessary to start the torrent of iron and high explosives toward Paris. By the time the first shell would reach its mark nine more would be on their way, stretched across the midnight sky at intervals of less than eight miles. And once started the stream would continue uninterrupted for two hours. The fascinated eyes of all the officers fastened themselves upon the key. None spoke.

"Well, well, gentlemen!" exclaimed the general brusquely, "what is the matter with you? You act as if you were at a funeral! Hans," turning to the orderly, "open the champagne there. Fill the glasses. Bumpers all, gentlemen, for the greatest inventor of all times, Herr von Heckmann, the inventor of the Relay Gun!"

The orderly sprang forward and hastily commenced uncorking bottles, while Von Heckmann turned away to the window.

"Here, this won't do, Schelling! You must liven

things up a bit!" continued the general to one of the officers. "This is a great occasion for all of us! Give me that bottle." He seized a magnum of champagne from the orderly and commenced pouring out the foaming liquid into the glasses beside the plates. Schelling made a feeble attempt at a joke at which the officers laughed loudly, for the general was a martinet and had to be humoured.

"Now, then," called out the general as he glanced toward the window, "Herr von Heckmann, we are going to drink your health! Officers of the First Artillery, I give you a toast—a toast which you will all remember to your dying day! Bumpers, gentlemen! No heel taps! I give you the health of 'Thanatos'—the leviathan of artillery, the winged bearer of death and destruction—and of its inventor, Herr von Heckmann. Bumpers, gentlemen!" The general slapped Von Heckmann upon the shoulder and drained his glass.

"'Thanatos!' Von Heckmann!" shouted the officers. And with one accord they dashed their goblets to the stone flagging upon which they stood.

"And now, my dear inventor," said the general, "to you belongs the honour of arousing 'Thanatos'

THE MAN WHO ROCKED THE EARTH

into activity. Are you ready, gentlemen? I warn you that when 'Thanatos' snores the rafters will ring."

Von Heckmann had stood with bowed head while the officers had drunk his health, and he now hesitatingly turned toward the little brass switch with its button of black rubber that glistened so innocently in the candlelight. His right hand trembled. He dashed the back of his left across his eyes. The general took out a large silver watch from his pocket. "Fifty-nine minutes past eleven," he announced. "At one minute past twelve Paris will be disembowelled. Put your finger on the button, my friend. Let us start the ball rolling."

Von Heckmann cast a glance almost of disquietude upon the faces of the officers who were leaning over the table in the intensity of their excitement. His elation, his exaltation, had passed from him. He seemed overwhelmed at the momentousness of the act which he was about to perform. Slowly his index finger crept toward the button and hovered half suspended over it. He pressed his lips together and was about to exert the pressure required to transmit the current of electricity to the discharging apparatus when unexpectedly there echoed through the night the sharp click of a horse's hoofs coming at a gallop down the village street. The group turned expectantly to the doorway.

An officer dressed in the uniform of an aide-de-camp of artillery entered abruptly, saluted, and produced from the inside pocket of his jacket a sealed envelope which he handed to the general. The interest of the officers suddenly centred upon the contents of the envelope. The general grumbled an oath at the interruption, tore open the missive, and held the single sheet which it contained to the candlelight.

"An armistice!" he cried disgustedly. His eye glanced rapidly over the page.

"*To the Major-General commanding the First Division of Artillery, Army of the Meuse:*
"An armistice has been declared, to commence at midnight, pending negotiations for peace. You will see that no acts of hostility occur until you receive notice that war is to be resumed.
"VON HELMUTH,
"Imperial Commissioner for War."

The officers broke into exclamations of impatience as the general crumpled the missive in his hand and cast it upon the floor.

"*Donnerwetter!*" he shouted. "Why were we

so slow? Curse the armistice!" He glanced at his watch. It already pointed to after midnight. His face turned red and the veins in his forehead swelled.

"To hell with peace!" he bellowed, turning back his watch until the minute hand pointed to five minutes to twelve. "To hell with peace, I say! Press the button, Von Heckmann!"

But in spite of the agony of disappointment which he now acutely experienced, Von Heckmann did not fire. Sixty years of German respect for orders held him in a viselike grip and paralyzed his arm.

"I can't," he muttered. "I can't."

The general seemed to have gone mad. Thrusting Von Heckmann out of the way, he threw himself into a chair at the end of the table and with a snarl pressed the black handle of the key.

The officers gasped. Hardened as they were to the necessities of war, no act of insubordination like the present had ever occurred within their experience. Yet they must all uphold the general; they must all swear that the gun was fired before midnight. The key clicked and a blue bead snapped at the switch. They held their breaths, looking through the window to the west.

At first the night remained still. Only the chirp of the crickets and the fretting of the aide-de-camp's horse outside the cottage could be heard. Then, like the grating of a coffee mill in a distant kitchen when one is just waking out of a sound sleep, they heard the faint, smothered whir of machinery, a sharper metallic ring of steel against steel followed by a gigantic detonation which shook the ground upon which the cottage stood and overthrew every glass upon the table. With a roar like the fall of a skyscraper the first shell hurled itself into the night. Half terrified the officers gripped their chairs, waiting for the second discharge. The reverberation was still echoing among the hills when the second detonation occurred, shortly followed by the third and fourth. Then, in intervals between the crashing explosions, a distant rumbling growl, followed by a shuddering of the air, as if the night were frightened, came up out of the west toward Paris, showing that the projectiles were at the top of their flight and going into action. A lake of yellow smoke formed in the pocket behind the hill where lay the redoubt in which "Thanatos" was snoring.

On the great race track of Longchamps, in the Bois

de Boulogne, the vast herd of cows, sheep, horses, and goats, collected together by the city government of Paris and attended by fifty or sixty shepherds especially imported from *les Landes*, had long since ceased to browse and had settled themselves down into the profound slumber of the animal world, broken only by an occasional bleating or the restless whinnying of a stallion. On the race course proper, in front of the grandstand and between it and the judge's box, four of these shepherds had built a small fire and by its light were throwing dice for coppers. They were having an easy time of it, these shepherds, for their flocks did not wander, and all that they had to do was to see that the animals were properly driven to such parts of the Bois as would afford proper nourishment.

"Well, *mes enfants*," exclaimed old Adrian Bannalec, pulling a turnip-shaped watch from beneath his blouse and holding it up to the firelight, "it's twelve o'clock and time to turn in. But what do you say to a cup of chocolate first?"

The others greeted the suggestion with approval, and going somewhere underneath the grandstand, Bannalec produced a pot filled with water, which he suspended with much dexterity over the fire upon the end of a pointed stick. The water began to boil almost immediately, and they were on the point of breaking their chocolate into it when, from what appeared to be an immense distance, through the air there came a curious rumble.

"What was that?" muttered Bannalec. The sound was followed within a few seconds by another, and after a similar interval by a third and fourth.

"There was going to be an armistice," suggested one of the younger herdsmen. He had hardly spoken before a much louder and apparently nearer detonation occurred.

"That must be one of our guns," said old Adrian proudly. "Do you hear how much louder it speaks than those of the Germans?"

Other discharges now followed in rapid succession, some fainter, some much louder. And then somewhere in the sky they saw a flash of flame, followed by a thunderous concussion which rattled the grandstand, and a great fiery serpent came soaring through the heavens toward Paris. Each moment it grew larger, until it seemed to be dropping straight toward them out of the sky, leaving a trail of sparks behind it.

"It's coming our way," chattered Adrian.

"God have mercy upon us!" murmured the others.

Rigid with fear, they stood staring with open mouths at the shell that seemed to have selected them for the object of its flight.

"God have mercy on our souls!" repeated Adrian after the others.

Then there came a light like that of a million suns. . . .

Alas for the wives and children of the herdsmen! And alas for the herds! But better that the eight core bombs projected by "Thanatos" through the midnight sky toward Paris should have torn the foliage of the Bois, destroyed the grandstands of Auteuil and Longchamps, with sixteen hundred innocent sheep and cattle, than that they should have sought their victims among the crowded streets of the inner city. Lucky for Paris that the Relay Gun had been sighted so as to sweep the metropolis from the west to the east, and that though each shell approached nearer to the walls than its preceding brother, none reached the ramparts. For with the discharge of the eighth shell and the explosion of the first core bomb filled with lyddite among the sleeping animals huddled on the turf in front of the grandstands, something happened which the poor shepherds did not see.

The watchers in the Eiffel Tower, seering the heavens with their searchlights for German planes and German dirigibles, saw the first core bomb bore through the sky from the direction of Verdun, followed by its seven comrades, and saw each bomb explode in the Bois below. But as the first shell shattered the stillness of the night and spread its sulphureous and death-dealing fumes among the helpless cattle, the watchers on the Tower saw a vast light burst skyward in the far-distant east.

Two miles up the road from the village of Champaubert, Karl Biedenkopf, a native of Hesse-Nassau and a private of artillery, was doing picket duty. The moonlight turned the broad highroad toward Epernay into a gleaming white boulevard down which he could see, it seemed to him, for miles. The air was soft and balmy, and filled with the odour of hay which the troopers had harvested "on behalf of the Kaiser." Across the road "Gretchen," Karl's mare, grazed ruminatively, while the picket himself sat on the stone wall by the roadside, smoking the

Bremen cigar which his corporal had given him after dinner.

The night was thick with stars. They were all so bright that at first he did not notice the comet which sailed slowly toward him from the northwest, seemingly following the line of the German intrenchments from Amiens, St.-Quentin, and Laon toward Rheims and Épernay. But the comet was there, dropping a long yellow beam of light upon the sleeping hosts that were beleaguering the outer ring of the French fortifications. Suddenly the repose of Biedenkopf's retrospections was abruptly disconcerted by the distant pounding of hoofs far down the road from Verdun. He sprang off the wall, took up his rifle, crossed the road, hastily adjusted "Gretchen's" bridle, leaped into the saddle, and awaited the night rider, whoever he might be. At a distance of three hundred feet he cried: "Halt!" The rider drew rein, hastily gave the countersign, and Biedenkopf, recognizing the aide-de-camp, saluted and drew aside.

"There goes a lucky fellow," he said aloud. "Nothing to do but ride up and down the roads, stopping wherever he sees a pleasant inn or a pretty face, spending money like water, and never risking a hair of his head."

It never occurred to him that maybe his was the luck. And while the aide-de-camp galloped on and the sound of his horse's hoofs grew fainter and fainter down the road toward the village, the comet came sailing swiftly on overhead, deluging the fortifications with a blinding orange-yellow light. It could not have been more than a mile away when Biedenkopf saw it. Instantly his trained eye recognized the fact that this strange round object shooting through the air was no wandering celestial body.

"*Ein Flieger!*" he cried hoarsely, staring at it in astonishment, knowing full well that no dirigible or aeroplane of German manufacture bore any resemblance to this extraordinary voyager of the air.

A hundred yards down the road his field telephone was attached to a poplar, and casting one furtive look at the Flying Ring he galloped to the tree and rang up the corporal of the guard. But at the very instant that his call was answered a series of terrific detonations shook the earth and set the wires roaring in the receiver, so that he could hear nothing. One

—two—three—four of them, followed by a distant answering boom in the west.

And then the whole sky seemed full of fire. He was hurled backward upon the road and lay half-stunned, while the earth discharged itself into the air with a roar like that of ten thousand shells exploding all together. The ground shook, groaned, grumbled, grated, and showers of boards, earth, branches, rocks, vegetables, tiles, and all sorts of unrecognizable and grotesque objects fell from the sky all about him. It was like a gigantic and never-ending mine, or series of mines, in continuous explosion, a volcano pouring itself upward out of the bowels of an incandescent earth. Above the ear-splitting thunder of the eruption he heard shrill cries and raucous shoutings. Mounted men dashed past him down the road, singly and in squadrons. A molten globe dropped through the branches of the poplar, and striking the hard surface of the road at a distance of fifty yards scattered itself like a huge ingot dropped from a blast furnace. Great clouds of dust descended and choked him. A withering heat enveloped him. . . .

It was noon next day when Karl Biedenkopf raised

his head and looked about him. He thought first there had been a battle. But the sight that met his eyes bore no resemblance to a field of carnage. Over his head he noticed that the uppermost branches of the poplar had been seared as by fire. The road looked as if the countryside had been traversed by a hurricane. All sorts of débris filled the fields and everywhere there seemed to be a thick deposit of blackened earth. Vaguely realizing that he must report for duty, he crawled, in spite of his bursting head and aching limbs, on all fours down the road toward the village.

But he could not find the village. There was no village there; and soon he came to what seemed to be the edge of a gigantic crater, where the earth had been uprooted and tossed aside as if by some huge convulsion of nature. Here and there masses of inflammable material smoked and flickered with red flames. His eyes sought the familiar outlines of the redoubts and fortifications, but found them not. And where the village had been there was a great cavern in the earth, and the deepest part of the cavern, or so it seemed to his half-blinded sight, was at about the point where the cottage had stood which his general had used as his headquarters, the spot where the night before that general had raised his glass of bubbling wine and toasted "Thanatos," the personification of death, and called his officers to witness that this was the greatest moment in the history of warfare, a moment that they would all remember to their dying day.

XII

THE shabby-genteel little houses of the Appian Way, in Cambridge, whose window-eyes with their blue-green lids had watched Bennie Hooker come and go, trudging back and forth to lectures and recitations, first as boy and then as man, for thirty years, must have blinked with amazement at the sight of the little professor as he started on the afterward famous Hooker Expedition to Labrador in search of the Flying Ring.

For the five days following Thornton's unexpected visit Bennie, existing without sleep and almost without food save for his staple of ready-to-serve chocolate, was the centre of a whirl of books, logarithms, and calculations in the University Library, and constituted himself an unmitigated, if respected, pest at the Cambridge Observatory. Moreover—and this was the most iconoclastic spectacle of all to his conservative pedagogical neighbours in the Appian Way—telegraph boys on bicycles kept rushing to and fro in a stream between the Hooker boarding-house and Harvard Square at all hours of the day and night.

For Bennie had lost no time and had instantly started in upon the same series of experiments to locate the origin of the phenomena which had shaken the globe as had been made use of by Professor von Schwenitz at the direction of General von Helmuth, the Imperial German Commissioner for War, at Mainz. The result had been approximately identical, and Hooker had satisfied himself that somewhere in the centre of Labrador his fellow-scientist—the discoverer of the Lavender Ray—was conducting the operations that had resulted in the dislocation of the earth's axis and retardation of its motion. Filled with a pure and unselfish scientific joy, it became his sole and immediate ambition to find the man who had done these things, to shake him by the hand, and to compare notes with him upon the now solved problems of thermic induction and of atomic disintegration.

But how to get there? How to reach him? For Prof. Bennie Hooker had never been a hundred miles from Cambridge in his life, and a journey to

Labrador seemed almost as difficult as an attempt to reach the pole. Off again then to the University Library, with pale but polite young ladies hastening to fetch him atlases, charts, guidebooks, and works dealing with sport and travel, until at last the great scheme unfolded itself to his mind—the scheme that was to result in the perpetuation of atomic disintegration for the uses of mankind and the subsequent alteration of civilization, both political and economic. Innocently, ingeniously, ingenuously, he mapped it all out. No one must know what he was about. Oh, no! He must steal away, in disguise if need be, and reach Pax alone. Three would be a crowd in that communion of scientific thought! He must take with him the notes of his own experiments, the diagrams of his apparatus, and his precious zirconium; and he must return with the great secret of atomic disintegration in his breast, ready, with the discoverer's permission, to give it to the dry and thirsty world. And then, indeed, the earth would blossom like the rose!

A strange sight, the start of the Hooker Expedition! Doctor Jelly's coloured housemaid had just thrown a pail of blue-gray suds over his front steps—it was

6:30 A. M.—and was on the point of resignedly kneeling and swabbing up the doctor's porch, when she saw the door of the professor's residence open cautiously and a curious human exhibit, the like of which had ne'er before been seen on sea or land, surreptitiously emerge. It was Prof. Bennie Hooker—disguised as a salmon fisherman!

Over a brand-new sportsman's knickerbocker suit of screaming yellow check he had donned an English mackintosh. On his legs were gaiters, and on his head a helmetlike affair of cloth with a visor in front and another behind, with eartabs fastened at the crown with a piece of black ribbon—in other words a "Glengarry." The suit had been manufactured in Harvard Square, and was a triumph of sartorial art on the part of one who had never been nearer to a real fisherman than a coloured fashion plate. However, it did suggest a sportsman of the variety usually portrayed in the comic supplements, and, to complete the picture, in Professor Hooker's hands and under his arms were yellow pigskin bags and rod cases, so that he looked like the show window of a harness store.

"Fo' de land sakes!" exclaimed the Jellys' coloured

maid, oblivious of her suds. "Fo' de Lawd! Am dat Perfesser Hookey?"

It was! But a new and glorified professor, with a soul thrilling to the joy of discovery and romance, with a flash in his eyes, and the savings of ten years in a large roll in his left-hand knickerbocker pocket.

Thus started the Hooker Expedition, which discovered the Flying Ring and made the famous report to the Smithsonian Institution after the disarmament of the nations. But could the nations have seen the expedition as it emerged from its boarding-house that September morning they would have rubbed their eyes.

With the utmost difficulty Prof. Bennie Hooker negotiated his bags and rod cases as far as Harvard Square, where, through the assistance of a friendly conductor with a sense of humour, he was enabled to board an electric surface car to the North Station.

Beyond the start up the River Moisie his imagination refused to carry him. But he had a faith that approximated certainty that over the Height of Land—just over the edge—he would find Pax and the Flying Ring. During all the period required for his experiments and preparations he had never once glanced at a newspaper or inquired as to the progress of the war that was rapidly exterminating the inhabitants of the globe. Thermic induction, atomic disintegration, the Lavender Ray, these were the Alpha, the Sigma, the Omega of his existence.

But meantime* the war had gone on with all its concomitant horror, suffering, and loss of life, and the representatives of the nations assembled at Washington had been feverishly attempting to unite upon the terms of a universal treaty that should end militarism and war forever. And thereafter, also, although Professor Hooker was sublimely unconscious of the fact, the celebrated conclave, known as Conference No. 2, composed of the best-known scientific men from every land, was sitting, perspiring, in the great lecture hall of the Smithsonian Institution, its members shouting at one another in a dozen different languages, telling each other what they did and didn't know, and becoming more and more confused and entangled in an underbrush of contradictory facts and observations and irreconcilable theories until they were making no progress whatever—which was precisely what the astute and plausible Count von

---
*Up to the date of the armistice.

Koenitz, the German Ambassador, had planned and intended.

The Flying Ring did not again appear, and in spite of the uncontroverted testimony of Acting-Consul Quinn, Mohammed Ben Ali el Bad, and a thousand others who had actually seen the Lavender Ray, people began gradually, almost unconsciously, to assume that the destruction of the Atlas Mountains had been the work of an unsuspected volcano and that the presence of the Flying Ring had been a coincidence and not the cause of the disruption. So the incident passed by and public attention refocussed itself upon the conflict on the plains of Châlons-sur-Marne. Only Bill Hood, Thornton, and a few others in the secret, together with the President, the Cabinet, and the members of Conference No. 1 and of Conference No. 2, truly apprehended the significance of what had occurred, and realized that either war or the human race must pass away forever. And no one at all, save only the German Ambassador and the Imperial German Commissioners, suspected that one of the nations had conceived and was putting into execution a plan designed to result in the acquirement of the secret of how the earth could be rocked and in the capture of the discoverer. For the *Sea Fox*, bearing the German expeditionary force, had sailed from Amsterdam twelve days after the conference held at Mainz between Professor von Schwenitz and General von Helmuth, and having safely rounded the Orkneys was now already well on its course toward Labrador. Bennie Hooker, however, was ignorant of all these things. Like an immigrant with a tag on his arm, he sat on the train which bore him toward Quebec, his ticket stuck into the band on his hat, dreaming of a transformer that wouldn't—couldn't—melt at only six thousand degrees.

When Professor Hooker awoke in his room at the hotel in Quebec the morning after his arrival there, he ate a leisurely breakfast, and having smoked a pipe on the terrace, strolled down to the wharves along the river front. Here to his disgust he learned that the Labrador steamer, the *Druro*, would not sail until the following Thursday—a three days' wait. Apparently Labrador was a less-frequented locality than he had supposed. He mastered his impatience, however, and discovering a library presided over by a highly intelligent graduate of Edinburgh, he became so interested in various profound treatises on physics which he discovered that he almost missed his boat.

Assisted by the head porter, and staggering under the weight of his new rod cases and other impedimenta, Bennie boarded the *Druro* on Thursday morning, engaged a stateroom, and purchased a ticket for Seven Islands, which is the nearest harbour to the mouth of the River Moisie. She was a large and comfortable river steamer of about eight hundred and fifty tons, and from her appearance belied the fact that she was the connecting link between civilization and the desolate and ice-clad wastes of the Far North, as in fact she was. The captain regarded Bennie with indifference, if not disrespect, grunted, and ascending to the pilot house blew the whistle. Quebec, with its teeming wharves and crowded shipping, overlooked by the cliffs that made Wolfe famous, slowly fell behind. Off their leeward bow the Isle of Orléans swung nearer and swept past, its neat homesteads inviting the weary traveller to pastoral repose. The river cleared. Low, farm-clad shores began to slip by. The few tourists and returning habitans settled themselves in the bow and made ready for their voyage.

There would have been much to interest the ordinary American traveller in this comparatively unfrequented corner of his native continent; but our salmon fisherman, having conveniently disposed of his baggage, immediately retired to his stateroom and, intent on saving time, proceeded, wholly oblivious of the *Druro*, to read passionately several exceedingly uninviting looking books which he produced from his valise. The *Druro*, quite as oblivious to Professor Hooker, proceeded on her accustomed way, passed by Tadousac, and made her first stop at the Godbout. Bennie, finding the boat no longer in motion, reappeared on deck under the mistaken impression that they had reached the end of the voyage, for he was unfamiliar with the topography of the St. Lawrence, and in fact had very vague ideas as to distances and the time required to traverse them by rail or boat.

At the Godbout the *Druro* dropped a habitan or two, a few boatloads of steel rods, crates of crockery and tobacco, and then thrust her bow out into the stream and steered down river, rounding at length the Pointe des Monts and winding in behind the Isles des Oeufs to the River Pentecoute, where she deposited some more habitans, including a priest in a black soutane, who somewhat incongruously was smoking a large cigar. Then, nosing through a fog bank and breaking out at last into sunlight again, she steamed across and put in past the Carousel, that picturesque and rocky headland, into Seven Islands Bay. Here she anchored, and, having discharged cargo, steamed out by the Grand Boule, where eighteen miles beyond the islands Bennie saw the pilot house of the old *St. Olaf*, of unhappy memory, just lifting above the water.

He had emerged from the retirement of his stateroom only on being asked by the steward for his ticket and learning that the *Druro* was nearing the end of her journey. For nearly two days he had been submerged in Soddy on The Interpretation of Radium. The *Druro* was running along a sandy, lowlying beach about half a mile offshore. They were nearing the mouth of a wide river. The volume of black fresh water from the Moisie rushed out into the St. Lawrence until it met the green sea water, causing a sharp demarcation of colour and a no less pronounced conflict of natural forces. For, owing to the pressure of the tide against the solid mass of the fresh stream, acres of water unexpectedly boiled on all sides, throwing geysers of foam twenty feet or more into the air, and then subsided. Off the point the engine bell rang twice, and the *Druro* came to a pause.

Bennie, standing in the bow, in his sportsman's cap and waterproof, hugging his rod cases to his breast, watched while a heterogeneous fleet of canoes, skiffs, and sailboats came racing out from shore, for the steamer does not land here, but hangs in the offing and lighters its cargo ashore. Leading the lot was a sort of whaleboat propelled by two oars on one side and one on the other, and in the sternsheets sat a rosy-cheeked, good-natured looking man with a smooth-shaven face who Bennie knew must be Malcolm Holliday.

"Hello, Cap!" shouted Holliday. "Any passengers?"

The captain from the pilot house waved contemptuously in Bennie's general direction.

"Howdy!" said Holliday. "What do you want? What can I do for you?"

"I thought I'd try a little salmon fishing," shrieked Bennie back at him.

Holliday shook his head. "Sorry," he bellowed· "river's leased. Besides, the officers* are here."

"Oh!" answered Bennie ruefully. "I didn't know. I supposed I could fish anywhere."

"Well, you can't!" snapped Holliday, puzzled by the little man's curious appearance.

"I suppose I can go ashore, can't I?" insisted Bennie somewhat indignantly. "I'll just take a camping trip then. I'd like to see the big salmon cache up at the forks if I can't do anything else."

Instantly Holliday scented something. "Another fellow after gold," he muttered to himself.

Just at that moment, the tide being at the ebb, a hundred acres of green water off the *Druro's* bow broke into whirling waves and jets of foam again. All about them, and a mile to seaward, these merry men danced by the score. Bennie thrilled at the beauty of it. The whaleboat containing Holliday was now right under the ship's bows.

"I want to look round anyhow," expostulated

---

*Along the St. Lawrence and the Labrador coast a salmon fisherman is always spoken of by natives and local residents as an "officer," the reason being that most of the sportsmen who visit these waters are English army officers. Hence salmon fishermen are universally termed "officers," and a habitan will describe the sportsmen who have rented a certain river as *"les officiers de la Moisie"* or *"les officiers de la Romaine."*

Bennie. "I've come all the way from Boston." He felt himself treated like a criminal, felt the suspicion in Holliday's eye.

The factor laughed. "In that case you certainly deserve sympathy." Then he hesitated. "Oh, well, come along," he said finally. "We'll see what we can do for you."

A rope ladder had been thrown over the side and one of the sailors now lowered Bennie's luggage into the boat. The professor followed, avoiding with difficulty stepping on his mackintosh as he climbed down the slippery rounds. Holliday grasped his hand and yanked him to a seat in the stern.

"Yes," he repeated, "if you've come all the way from Boston I guess we'll have to put you up for a few days anyway."

A crate of canned goods, a parcel of mail, and a huge bundle of newspapers were deposited in the bow. Holliday waved his hand. The *Druro* churned the water and swung out into midstream again. Bennie looked curiously after her. To the north lay a sandy shore dotted by a scraggy forest of dwarf spruce and birch. A few fishing huts and a mass of wooden shanties fringed the forest. To the east, seaward, many miles down that great stretch of treacherous, sullen river waited a gray bank of fog. But overhead the air was crystalline with that sparkling, cratchy brilliance that is found only in northern climes. Nature seemed hard, relentless. With his feet entangled in rod cases Professor Hooker wondered for a moment what on earth he was there for, landing on this inhospitable coast. Then his eyes sought the genial face of Malcolm Holliday and hope sprang up anew. For there is that about this genial frontiersman that draws all men to him alike, be they Scotch or English, Canadian habitans or Montagnais, and he is the king of the coast, as his father was before him, or as was old Peter McKenzie, the head factor, who incidentally cast the best salmon fly ever thrown east of Montreal or south of Ungava. Bennie found comfort in Holliday's smile, and felt toward him as a child does toward its mother.

They neared shore and ran alongside a ramshackle pier, up the slippery poles of which Bennie was instructed to clamber. Then, dodging rotten boards and treacherous places, he gained the sand of the beach and stood at last on Labrador. A group of Montagnais picked up the professor's luggage and, headed by Holliday, they started for the latter's house. It was a strange and amusing landing of an expedition the results of which have revolutionized the life of the inhabitants of the entire globe. No such inconspicuous event has ever had so momentous a conclusion. And now when Malcolm Holliday makes his yearly trip home to Quebec, to report to the firm of Holliday Brothers, who own all the nets far east of Anticosti, he spends hours at the Club des Voyageurs, recounting in detail all the circumstances surrounding the arrival of Professor Hooker and how he took him for a gold hunter.

"Anyhow," he finishes, "I knew he wasn't a salmon fisherman in spite of his rods and cases, for he didn't know a Black Dose from a Thunder and Lightning or a Jock Scott, and he thought you could catch salmon with a worm!"

It was true wholly. Bennie did suppose one killed the king of game fish as he had caught minnows in his childhood, and his geologic researches in the Harvard Library had not taught him otherwise. Neither had his tailor.

"My dear fellow," said Holliday as they smoked their pipes on the narrow board piazza at the Post, "of course I'll help you all I can, but you've come at a bad season of the year all round. In the first place, you'll be eaten alive by black flies, gnats, and mosquitoes." He slapped vigorously as he spoke. "And you'll have the devil of a job getting canoe men. You see all the Montagnais are down here at the settlement 'making their mass.' Once a year they leave the hunting grounds up by the Divide and beyond and come down river to *'faire la messe'*—it's a sacred duty with 'em. They're very religious, as you probably know—a fine lot, too, take 'em altogether, gentle, obedient, industrious, polite, cheerful, and fair to middling honest. They have a good deal of French blood—a bit diluted, but it's there."

"Can't I get a few to go along with me?" asked Bennie anxiously.

"That's a question," answered the factor meditatively. "You know how the birds—how caribou —migrate every year. Well, these Montagnais are just like them. They have a regular routine. Each man has a line of traps of his own, all the way up to the Height of Land. They all go up river in the autumn with their winter's supply of pork, flour, tea, powder, lead, axes, files, rosin to mend their canoes, and castoreum—made out of beaver glands, you know—to take away the smell of their hands from the baited traps. They go up in families, six or seven canoes together, and as each man reaches his own territory his canoe drops out of the procession and he makes a camp for his wife and babies. Then he spends the winter—six or seven months—in the woods following his line of traps. By and by the ice goes out and he begins to want some society. He hasn't seen a priest for ten months or so, and he's afraid of the *loup-garou*, for all I know. So he comes down river, takes his Newport season here at Moisie, and goes to mass and staves off the *loup-garou*. They're all here now. Maybe you can get a couple to go up river and maybe you can't."

Then observing Bennie's crestfallen expression, he added:

"But we'll see. Perhaps you can get Marc St. Ange and Edouard Moreau, both good fellows. They've made their mass and they know the country from here to Ungava. There's Marc now—*Venez ici, Marc St. Ange.*" A swarthy, lithe Montagnais was coming down the road, and Holliday addressed him rapidly in habitan French: "This gentleman wishes to go up river to the forks to see the big cache. Will you go with him?"

The Montagnais bowed to Professor Hooker and pondered the suggestion. Then he gesticulated toward the north and seemed to Bennie to be telling a long story.

Holliday laughed again. "Marc says he will go," he commented shortly. "But he says also that if the Great Father of the Marionettes is angry he will come back."

"What does he mean by that?" asked Bennie.

"Why, when the aurora borealis—Northern Lights—plays in the sky the Indians always say that the 'marionettes are dancing.' About four weeks ago we had some electrical disturbances up here and a kind of an earthquake. It scared these Indians silly. There was a tremendous display, almost like a volcano. It beat anything I ever saw, and I've been here fifteen years. The Indians said the Father of the Marionettes was angry because they didn't dance enough to suit him, and that he was making them dance. Then some of them caught a glimpse of a shooting star, or a comet, or something, and called it the Father of the Marionettes. They had quite a time—held masses, and so on—and were really cut up. But the thing is over now, except for the regular, ordinary display."

"When can they be ready?" inquired Bennie eagerly.

"To-morrow morning," replied Holliday. "Marc will engage his uncle. They're all right. Now how about an outfit? But don't talk any more about salmon. I know what you're after—it's *gold!*"

The moon was still hanging low over the firs at four o'clock the next morning when three black and silent shadows emerged from the factor's house and made their way, cautiously and with difficulty, across the sand to where a canoe had been run into the riffles of the beach. Marc came first, carrying a sheet-iron stove with a collapsible funnel; then his Uncle Edouard, shouldering a bundle consisting of a tent and a couple of sacks of flour and pork; and lastly Professor Hooker with his mackintosh and rifle, entirely unaware of the fact that his careful guides had removed all the cartridges from his luggage lest he should shoot too many caribou and so spoil the winter's food supply. It was cold, almost frosty. In the black flood of the river the stars burned with a chill, wavering light. Bennie put on his mackintosh with a shiver. The two guides quietly piled the luggage in the centre of the canoe, arranged a seat for their passenger, picked up their paddles, shoved off, and took their places in bow and stern.

No lights gleamed in the windows of Moisie. The lap of the ripples against the birch side of the canoe, the gurgle of the water round the paddle blades, and the rush of the bow as, after it had paused on the withdraw, it leaped forward on the stroke, were the only sounds that broke the deathlike silence of the semi-arctic night. Bennie struck a match, and it flared red against the black water as he lit his pipe, but he felt a great stirring within his little breast, a great courage to dare, to do, for he was off, really off, on his great hunt, his search for the secret that would remake the world. With the current whispering against its sides the canoe swept in a wide circle to midstream. The moon was now partially obscured behind the treetops. To the east a faint glow made the horizon seem blacker than ever. Ahead the wide waste of the dark river seemed like an engulfing chasm. Drowsiness enwrapped Professor Hooker, a drowsiness intensified by the rythmic swinging of the paddles and the pile of bedding against which he reclined. He closed his eyes, content to be driven onward toward the region of his hopes, content almost to fall asleep.

"Hi!" suddenly whispered Marc St. Ange. "*Voilà! Le père des marionettes!*"

Bennie awoke with a start that almost upset the canoe. The blood rushed to his face and sang in his ears.

"Where?" he cried. "Where?"

"*Au nord*," answered Marc. "*Mais il descend!*"

Professor Hooker stared in the direction of Marc's uplifted paddle. Was he deceived? Was the wish father to the thought? Or did he really see at an immeasurable distance upon the horizon a quickly dying trail of orange-yellow light? He rubbed his eyes—his heart beating wildly under his sportsman's suiting. But the north was black beyond the coming dawn.

Old Edouard grunted.

"*Vous êtes fou!*" he muttered to his nephew, and drove his paddle deep into the water.

Day broke with staccato emphasis. The sun swung

up out of Europe and burned down upon the canoe with a heat so equatorial in quality that Bennie discarded both his mackintosh and his sporting jacket. All signs of human life had disappeared from the distant banks of the river and the bow of the canoe faced a gray-blue flood emerging from a wilderness of scrubby trees. A few gulls flopped their way coastward, and at rare intervals a salmon leaped and slashed the slow-moving surface into a boiling circle; but for the rest their surroundings were as set, as immobile, as the painted scenery of a stage, save where the current swept the scattered promontories of the shore. But they moved steadily north. So wearied was Bennie with the unaccustomed light and fresh air that by ten o'clock he felt the day must be over, although the sun had not yet reached the zenith. Unexpectedly Marc and Edouard turned the canoe quietly into a shallow, and beached her on a spit of white sand. In three minutes Edouard had a small fire snapping, and handed Bennie a cup of tea. How wonderful it seemed—a genuine elixir! And then he felt the stab of a mosquito, and putting up his hand found it blotched with blood. And the black flies came also. Soon the professor was tramping up and down, waving his handkerchief and clutching wildly at the air. Then they pushed off again.

The sun dropped westward as they turned bend after bend, disclosing ever the same view beyond. Shadows of rocks and trees began to jut across the eddies. A great heron, as big as an ostrich, or so he seemed, arose awkwardly and flapped off, trailing yards of legs behind him. Then Bennie put on first his jacket and then his mackintosh. He realized that his hands were numb. The sun was now only a foot or so above the sky line.

This time it was Marc who grunted and thrust the canoe toward the river's edge with a sideways push. It grounded on a belt of sand and they dragged it ashore. Bennie, who had been looking forward to the night with vivid apprehension, now discovered to his great happiness that the chill was keeping away the black flies. Joyfully he assisted in gathering dry sticks, driving tent pegs, and picking reindeer moss for bedding. Then as darkness fell Edouard fried eggs and bacon, and with their boots off and their stockinged feet toasting to the blaze the three men ate as becomes men who have laboured fifteen hours in the open air. They drank tin cups of scalding tea, a pint at a time, and found it good; and they smoked their pipes with their backs propped against the tree trunks and found it heaven. Then as the stars came out and the woods behind them snapped with strange noises, Edouard took his pipe from his mouth.

"It's getting cold," said he. "The marionettes will dance to-night."

Bennie heard him as if across a great, yawning gulf. Even the firelight seemed hundreds of yards away. The little professor was "all in," and he sat with his chin dropped again to his chest, until he heard Marc exclaim:

"*Voilà! Elles dansent!*"

He raised his eyes. Just across the black, silent sweep of the river three giant prismatic searchlights were playing high toward the polestar, such searchlights as the gods might be using in some monstrous game. They wavered here and there, shifting and dodging, faded and sprang up again, till Bennie, dizzy, closed his eyes. The lights were still dancing in the north as he stumbled to his couch of moss.

"*Toujour les marionettes!*" whispered Marc gently, as he might to a child. "*Bon soir, monsieur.*"

The tent was hot and dazzling white above his

head when low voices, footsteps, and the clink of tin against iron aroused the professor from a profound coma. The guides had already loaded the canoe and were waiting for him. The sun was high. Apologetically he pulled on his boots, and stepping to the sand dashed the icy water into his face. His muscles groaned and rasped. His neck refused to respond to his desires with its accustomed elasticity. But he drank his tea and downed his scrambled eggs with an enthusiasm unknown in Cambridge, Massachusetts. Marc gave him a hand into the canoe and they were off. The day had begun.

The river narrowed somewhat and the shores grew more rocky. At noon they lunched on another sandspit. At sunset they saw a caribou. Night came. "Always the marionettes." Thus passed nine days —like a dream to Bennie; and then came the first adventure.

It was about four o'clock on the afternoon of the tenth day of their trip up the Moisie when Marc suddenly stopped paddling and gazed intently shoreward. After a moment he said something in a low tone to Edouard, and they turned the canoe and drove it rapidly toward a small cove half hidden by rocks. Bennie, straining his eyes, could see nothing at first, but when the canoe was but ten yards from shore he caught sight of the motionless figure of a man, lying on his face with his head nearly in the water. Marc turned him over gently, but the limbs fell limp, one leg at a grotesque angle to the knee. Bennie saw instantly that it was broken. The Indian's face was white and drawn, no doubt with pain.

"*Il est mort!*" said Marc slowly, crossing himself.

Edouard shrugged his shoulders and fetched a small flask of brandy from the professor's sack. Forcing open the jaws, he poured a few drops into the man's mouth. The Indian choked and opened his eyes. Edouard grunted.

"*La jeunesse pense qu'elle sait tout!*" he remarked scornfully.

Thus they found Nichicun, without whom Bennie might never have accomplished the object of his quest. It took three days to nurse the half-dead and altogether starved Montagnais back to life, but he received the tenderest care. Marc shot a young caribou and gave him the blood to drink, and made a ragout to put the flesh back on his bones. Meanwhile the professor slept long hours on the moss and took a much-needed rest; and by degrees they learned from Nichicun the story of his misfortune—the story that forms a part of the chronicle of the expedition, which can be read at the Smithsonian Institution.

He was a Montagnais, he said, with a line of traps to the northeast of the Height of Land, and last winter he had had very bad luck indeed. There had been less and less in his traps and he had seen no caribou. So he had taken his wife, who was sick, and had gone over into the Nascopee country for food, and there his wife had died. He had made up his mind very late in the season to come down to Moisie and make his mass and get a new wife, and start a fresh line of traps in the autumn. All the other Montagnais had descended the river in their canoes long before, so he was alone. His provisions had given out and he saw no caribou. He began to think he would surely starve to death. And then one evening, on the point just above their present camp, he had seen a caribou and shot it, but he had been too weak to take good aim and had only broken its shoulder. It lay kicking among the boulders, pushing itself along by its hind legs, and he had feared that it would escape. In his haste to reach it he had slipped on a wet rock and fallen and broken his leg. In spite of the pain he had crawled on, and then had taken place a wild, terrible fight for life between the dying man and the dying beast.

He could not remember all that had occurred—he had been kicked, gored, and bitten; but finally he had got a grip on its throat and slashed it with his knife. Then, lying there on the ground beside it, he drank its blood and cut off the raw flesh in strips for food. Finally one day he had crawled to the river for water and had fainted.

The professor and his guides made for the Indian a hut of rocks and bark, and threw a great pile of moss into the corner of it for him to lie on. They carved a splint for his leg and bound it up, and cut a huge heap of firewood for him, smoking caribou meat and hanging it up in the hut. Somebody would come up river and find him, or if not, the three men would pick him up on their return. For this was right and the law of the woods. But never a word of particular interest to Prof. Bennie Hooker did Nichicun speak until the night before their departure, although the reason and

THE MAN WHO ROCKED THE EARTH 165

manner of his speaking were natural enough. It happened as follows: but first it should be said that the Nascopees are an ignorant and barbarous tribe, dirty and treacherous, upon whom the Montagnais look down with contempt and scorn. They do not even wear civilized clothes, and their ways are not the ways of *les bons sauvages*. They have no priests; they do not come to the coast; and the Montagnais will not mingle with them. Thus it bespoke the hunger of Nichicun that he was willing to go into their country.

As he sat round the fire with Marc and Edouard on that last night, Nichicun spoke his mind of the Nascopees, and Marc translated freely for Bennie's edification.

No, the injured Montagnais told them, the Nascopees were not nice; they were dirty. They ate decayed food and they never went to mass. Moreover, they were half-witted. While he was there they were all planning to migrate for the most absurd reason—what do you suppose? Magic! They claimed the end of the world was coming! Of course it was coming some time. But they said now, right away. But why? Because the marionettes were dancing so much. And they had seen the Father of the Marionettes floating in the sky and making thunder! Fools! But the strangest thing of all, they said they could hunt no longer, for they were afraid to cross something—an iron serpent that stung with fire if you touched it, and killed you! What foolishness! An iron serpent! But he had asked them and they had sworn on the holy cross that it was true.

Bennie listened with a chill creeping up his spine. But it would never do to hint what this disclosure meant to him. Between puffs of his pipe he asked casual, careless questions of Nichicun. These Nascopees, for instance, how far off might their land be? And where did they assert this extraordinary serpent of iron to be? Were there rivers in the Nascopee country? Did white men ever go there? All these things the wounded Montagnais told him. It appeared, moreover, that the Rassini River was near the Nascopee territory, and that it flowed into the Moisie only seven miles above the camp. All that night the marionettes danced in Bennie's brain.

Next morning they propped Nichicun on his bed of moss, laid a rifle and a box of matches beside him, and bade him farewell. At the mouth of the Rassini River Prof. Bennie Hooker held up his hand and announced that he was going to the Nascopee country. The canoe halted abruptly. Old Edouard declared that they had been engaged only to go to the big cache, and that their present trip was merely by way of a little excursion to see the river. They had no supplies for such a journey, no proper amount of ammunition. No, they would deposit the professor on the nearest sandbar if he wished, but they were going back.

Bennie arose unsteadily in the canoe and dug into his pocket, producing a roll of gold coin. Two hundred and fifty dollars he promised them if they would take him to the nearest tribe of Nascopees; five hundred if they could find the Iron Serpent.

"*Bien!*" exclaimed both Indians without a moment's hesitation, and the canoe plunged forward up the Rassini.

Once more a dreamlike succession of brilliant, frosty days; once more the star-studded sky in which always the marionettes danced. And then at last the great falls of the Rassini, beyond which no white man had gone. They hid the canoe in the bushes and placed beneath it the iron stove and half their supply of food. Then they plunged into the brush, eastward. Bennie had never known such grueling work and heartbreaking fatigue; and the clouds of flies pursued them venomously and with unrelenting persistence. At first they had to cut their way through acres of brush, and then the land rose and they saw before them miles of swamp and barren land dotted with dwarf trees and lichen-grown rocks. Here it was easier and they made better time; but the professor's legs ached and his rifle wore a red bruise on his shoulder. And then after five days of torment they came upon the Iron Rail. It ran in almost a direct line from northwest to southwest, with hardly a waver, straight over the barrens and through the forests of scrub, with a five-foot clearing upon either side. At intervals it was elevated to a height of eight or ten inches upon insulated iron braces. Both Marc and Edouard stared at in wonder, while Bennie made them a little speech.

It was, he said, a thing called a "monorail," made by a man who possessed strange secrets concerning the earth and the properties of matter. That man lived over the Height of Land toward Ungava. He was a good man and would not harm other good men. But he was a great magician—if you believed in magic. On the rail undoubtedly he ran something called a gyroscopic engine, and carried his stores and machinery into the wilderness. The Nascopees were not such fools after all, for here was the something they feared to cross—the iron serpent that bit and killed. Let them watch while he made it bite. He allowed his rifle to fall against the rail, and instantly a shower of blue sparks flashed from it as the current leaped into the earth.

Bennie counted out twenty-five golden eagles and handed them to Edouard. If they followed the rail to its source he would, he promised, on their return to civilization give them as much again. Without more ado the Indians lifted their packs and swung off to the northwest along the line of the rail. The stock of Prof. Bennie Hooker had risen in their estimation. On they ploughed across the barrens, through swamps, over the quaking muskeg, into the patches of scrub growth where the short branches slapped their faces, but always they kept in sight of the rail.

The extraordinary announcement, transmitted from various European news agencies, that an attempt had been made by the general commanding the First Artillery Division of the German Army of the Meuse to violate the armistice, had caused a profound sensation, particularly as the attempt to destroy Paris had been prevented only by the sudden appearance of the same mysterious Flying Ring that had shortly before caused the destruction of the Atlas Mountains and the flooding of the Sahara Desert by the Mediterranean Sea.

The advent of the Flying Ring on this second occasion had been noted by several hundred thousand persons, both soldiers and non-combatants. At about the hour of midnight, as if to observe whether the warring nations intended sincerely to live up to their agreement and bring about an actual cessation of hostilities, the Ring had appeared out of the north and, floating through the sky, had followed the lines of the belligerents from Brussels to Verdun and southward. The blinding yellow light that it had projected toward the earth had roused the soldiers sleeping in their intrenchments and caused great consternation all along the line of fortifications, as it was universally supposed that the director of its flight intended to annihilate the combined armies of

France, England, Germany, and Belgium. But the Ring had sailed peacefully along, three thousand feet aloft, deluging the countryside with its dazzling light, sending its beams into the casemates of the huge fortresses of the Rhine and the outer line of the French fortifications, searching the redoubts and trenches, but doing no harm to the sleeping armies that lay beneath it; until at last the silence of the night had been broken by the thunder of "Thanatos," and in the twinkling of an eye the Lavender Ray had descended, to turn the village of Champaubert into the smoking crater of a dying volcano. The entire division of artillery had been annihilated, with the exception of a few stragglers, and of the Relay Gun naught remained but a distorted puddle of steel and iron.

Long before the news of the horrible retribution visited by the master of the Ring upon Treitschke, the major-general of artillery, and the inventor, Von Heckmann, had reached the United States, Bill Hood, sitting in the wireless receiving station of the Naval Observatory at Georgetown, had received through the ether a message from his mysterious correspondent in the north that sent him hurrying to the White House. Pax had called the Naval Observatory and had trans-

172 THE MAN WHO ROCKED THE EARTH

mitted the following ultimatum, repeating it, as was his custom, three times:

"*To the President of the United States and to All Mankind:*

"I have put the nations to the test and found them wanting. The solemn treaty entered into by the ambassadors of the belligerent nations at Washington has been violated. My attempt by harmless means to compel the cessation of hostilities and the abolition of war has failed. I cannot trust the nations of the earth. Their selfishness, their bloodthirstiness, and greed, will inevitably prevent their fulfilling their agreements with me or keeping the terms of their treaties with one another, which they regard, as they themselves declare, merely as 'scraps of paper.' The time has come for me to compel peace. I am the dictator of human destiny and my will is law. War shall cease. On the 10th day of September I shall shift the axis of the earth until the North Pole shall be in the region of Strassburg and the South Pole in New Zealand. The habitable zone of the earth will be hereafter in South Africa, South and Central America, and regions now unfrequented by man. The nations must migrate and a new life in which war is unknown must begin upon the globe. This is my last message to the human race.

PAX."

The conference of ambassadors summoned by the President to the White House that afternoon exhibited a character in striking contrast with the first, at which Von Koenitz and the ambassadors from France, Russia, and England had had their memorable disagreement. It was a serious, apprehensive, and subdued group of gentlemen that gathered round the great mahogany table in the Cabinet chamber to debate what course of action the nations should pursue to avert the impending calamity to mankind. For that Pax could shift the axis of the earth, or blow the globe clean out of its orbit into space, if he chose to do so, no one doubted any longer.

And first it fell as the task of the ambassador representing the Imperial German Commissioners to assure his distinguished colleagues that his nation disavowed and denied all responsibility for the conduct of General Treitschke in bombarding Paris after the hour set for the armistice. It was unjust and contrary to the dictates of reason, he argued, to hold the government of a nation comprising sixty-five millions of human beings and five millions of armed men accountable for the actions of a single individual. He spoke passionately, eloquently, persuasively, and at the conclusion of his speech the ambassadors present were forced to acknowledge that what he said was true, and to accept without reservation his plausible assurances that the Imperial German Commissioners had no thought but to coöperate with the other governments in bringing about a lasting peace such as Pax demanded.

But the immediate question was, had not the time for this gone by? Was it not too late to convince the master of the Flying Ring that his orders would be obeyed? Could anything be done to avert the calamity he threatened to bring upon the earth—to prevent the conversion of Europe into a barren waste of ice fields? For Pax had announced that he had spoken for the last time and that the fate of Europe was sealed. All the ambassadors agreed that a general European immigration was practically impossible; and as a last resort it was finally decided to transmit to Pax, through the Georgetown station, a wireless message signed by all the ambassadors of the belligerent nations, solemnly agreeing within one week to disband their armies and to destroy all their munitions and implements of war. This message was delivered to Hood, with instructions for its immediate delivery. All that afternoon and evening the operator sat in the observatory, calling over and over again the three letters that marked mankind's only communication with the controller of its destiny:

"PAX—PAX—PAX!"

But no answer came. For long, weary hours Hood waited, his ears glued to the receivers. An impenetrable silence surrounded the master of the Ring. Pax had spoken. He would say no more. Late that night Hood reluctantly returned to the White House and informed the President that he was unable to deliver the message of the nations.

And meantime Prof. Bennie Hooker, with Marc and Edouard, struggled across the wilderness of Labrador, following the Iron Rail that led to the hiding-place of the master of the world.

The terrible fate of the German expeditionary force is too well known to require comment. As has been already told, the *Sea Fox* had sailed from Amsterdam twelve days after the conference in the War Office at Mainz between General von Helmuth and Professor von Schwenitz. Once north of the Orkneys it had encountered fair weather, and it had reached Hamilton Inlet in ten days without mishap, and with the men and animals in the best of condition. At Rigolet the men had disembarked and loaded their howitzers, mules, and supplies upon the flat-bottomed barges brought with them for that purpose. Thirty French and Indian guides had been engaged, and five days later the expedition, towed by the powerful motor launches, had started up the river toward the chain of lakes lying northwest toward Ungava. Every one was in the best of spirits and everything moved with customary German precision like clockwork. Nothing had been forgotten, not even the pungent invention of a Berlin chemist to discourage mosquitoes. Without labour, without anxiety, the fourteen barges bored through the swift currents and at last reached a great lake that lay like a silver mirror for miles about them. The moon rose and turned the boats into weird shapes as they ploughed through the gray mists—a strange and terrible sight for the Nascopees lurking in the underbrush along the shore. And while the men smoked and sang "Die Wacht am Rhein," listening to the trill of the ripples against the bows, the foremost motorboat grounded.

The momentum of the barge immediately following

could not be checked, and she in turn drove into what seemed to be a mud bank. At about the same instant the other barges struck bottom. Intense excitement and confusion prevailed among the members of the expedition, since they were almost out of sight of land and the draft of the motorboats was only nineteen inches. But no efforts could move the barges from where they were. All night long the propellers churned the gleaming water of the lake to foam, but without result. Each and every barge and boat was hard and fast aground, and when the gray daylight came stealing across the lake there was no lake to be seen, only a reeking marsh, covered for miles with a welter of green slime and decaying vegetable matter across which it would seem no human being or animal could flounder. As far as the eye could reach lay only a blackish ooze. And with the sun came millions of mosquitoes and flies, and drove the men and mules frantic with their stings.

Only one man, Ludwig Helmer, a gun driver from Potsdam, survived. Half mad with the flies and nearly naked, he found his way somehow across the quaking bog, after all his comrades had died of thirst, and reached a tribe of Nascopees, who took him to the coast. A great explosion, they told him, had torn the River Nascopee from its bed and diverted its course. The lakes that it fed had all dried up.

Blinded by perspiration, sweltering under the heavy burden of their outfit, goaded almost to frenzy by the black flies and mosquitoes, Hooker and Marc and Edouard staggered through the brush, following the monorail. They had already reached the summit of the Height of Land and where now working down the northern slope in the direction of Ungava. The land was barren beyond the imagination of the unimaginative Bennie. Small dwarfed trees struggled for a footing amid the lichen-covered outcroppings and sun-dried moss of the hollows. The slightest rise showed mile upon mile of great waste undulating interminably in every direction. The heat shimmering off the rocks was almost suffocating. At noon on September 10th they threw themselves into the shade of a narrow ledge, boiled some tea, and smoked their pipes, wildly fanning the air to drive away the swarms of insects that attacked them.

Hooker was half drunk from lack of sleep and water. Already once or twice he had caught himself wandering when talking to Marc and Edouard. The whole thing was like a horrible, disgusting nightmare. And then he suddenly became aware that the two Indians were staring intently through the clouds of mosquitoes over the tree tops to the eastward. Through the sweat that trickled into his eyes he tried to make out what they could see. But he could discern nothing except mosquitoes. And then he thought he saw a mosquito larger than all the others. He waved at it, but it remained where it was. A slight breeze momentarily wafted the swarm away, and he still saw the big mosquito hovering over the horizon. Then he heard Marc cry out:

"*Quelque chose vol en l'air!*"

He rubbed the moisture out of his eyes and stared at the mosquito, which was growing bigger every minute. With the velocity of a projectile, this monstrous insect, or whatever it was, came sweeping up behind them from the Height of Land, soaring into the zenith in a great parabola, until with a shiver of excitement Bennie recognized that it was the Flying Ring.

"It's him," he chattered emphatically, if ungrammatically.

Marc and Edouard nodded.

"*Oui, oui!*" they cried in unison. "*C'est celui que vous cherchez!*"

"*Il retourne chez lui,*" said Marc.

And then Bennie, without offering any explanation, found himself dancing up and down upon the rocks in the dizzying sun, waving his hat and shouting to the Father of the Marionettes. What he shouted he never knew. And Marc and Edouard both shouted, too. But the master of the Ring heard them not, or if he heard he paid them no attention. Nearer and nearer came the Ring, until Bennie could see the gleaming cylinder of its great steel circle. At a distance of about two miles it swept through the air over a low ridge, and settled toward the earth in the direction of Ungava.

"He only goes ten mile maybe," announced Marc confidently. "*Un petit bout de chemin.* We get there to-night."

On they struggled beside the Rail, but now hope ran high. Bennie sang and whistled, unmindful of the mosquitoes and black flies that renewed their attacks with unremitting ferocity. The sun lowered itself into the pine trees, shooting dazzling shafts through the low branches, and then sank in a welter of crimson-yellow light. The sky turned gray in the east; faint stars twinkled through the quivering waves that still shook from the overheated rocks. It turned cold and the mosquitoes departed. Hugging the Rail, they staggered on, now over shaking muskeg, now through thickets of tangled brush, now on great ledges of barren rock, and then across caribou barrens knee-deep in dry and crackling moss. Darkness fell and prudence dictated that they should make camp. But in their excitement they trudged on, until presently a pale glow behind the dwarfed trees showed that the moon was rising. They boiled the water, made tea, and cooked some biscuits. Soon they could see to pursue their way.

"'Most there now," encouraged Marc.

Presently, instead of descending, they found the land was rising again, and forcing their way through the undergrowth they struggled up a rocky hillside, perhaps three hundred feet in height. Marc was in the lead, with Bennie a few feet behind him. As they reached the crest the Indian turned and pointed to something in front of him that Bennie was unable to distinguish.

"*Nous sommes arrivees,*" he announced.

With his heart thumping from the exertion of the climb, Bennie crawled up beside his guide and found himself confronted by a strong barbed-wire entanglement affixed to iron stanchions firmly imbedded in the rocks. They were on the top of a ridge that dropped away abruptly at their feet into a valley, perhaps a mile in width, terminating on the other side in perpendicular cliffs, estimated by Bennie to be about eight hundred or a thousand feet in height. Although the entanglement was by no means impassable, it was a distinct obstacle and one they preferred to tackle by daylight. Moreover, it indicated that their company was undesired. They were in the presence of an unknown quantity, the master of the Flying Ring. Whether he was a malign or a benevolent influence, this Father of the Marionettes, they could not tell.

With his back propped against a small spruce Bennie focused his glasses upon dim shapes barely discernible in the midst of the valley. He was thrilled by a deep excitement, a strange fear. What would he see? What mysteries would those vague forms disclose? The shadows cast by the cliffs and a light mist gathering in the low ground made it difficult to see; and then, even as he looked, the moon rose higher and shone through something in the middle of the valley that looked like a tall, grisly skeleton. It seemed to have legs and arms, an odd mushroom-shaped head, and endless ribs. Below and at its feet were other and vaguer shapes—flat domes or cupolas, bombproofs perhaps, buildings of some sort—Pax's home beyond peradventure.

As he looked through the glasses at the skeleton-like tower Bennie had an extraordinary feeling of having seen it all before somewhere. As in a long-forgotten dream he remembered Tesla's tower near Smithtown, on Long Island. And this was Tesla's tower, naught else! It is a strange thing, how at great crises of our lives come feelings of anticipatory knowledge. There is, indeed, nothing new under the sun; else had Bennie been more afraid. As it was, he saw only Tesla's Smithtown tower with its head like a young mushroom. And at the same time there flashed into his memory: "Childe Harold to the Dark Tower Came." Over and over he repeated it mechanically, feeling that he might be one of those of whom the poet had sung. Yet he had not read the lines for years:

> *Burningly it came on me all at once,*
> *This was the place! . . .*
> *What in the midst lay but the Tower itself?*

His eyes searched the shadows round the base of the tower, for his ears had already caught a faint, almost inaudible throbbing that seemed to grow from moment to moment. There certainly was a dull vibration in the air, a vibration like the distant hum of machinery. Suddenly old Edouard touched Bennie upon the shoulder.

"*Regardez!*" he whispered.

Some transformation was happening in the hood of the tower. From a black opaque object it began to turn a dull red and to diffuse a subdued glow, while the hum turned into a distinct whir.

Bennie became almost hysterical with excitement.

Soon the hood of the tower had turned white and the glow had increased until the whole valley was lit up with a suffused and gentle light. The Ring could be distinctly seen about half a mile away, resting upon a huge circular support.

"*C'est le feu!*" grunted Marc. "*C'est ainsi que l'on fait danser les marionettes!*"

There was no doubt that the hood of the tower was in fact white hot, for the perpendicular cliffs of the mountain across the valley sharply reflected the light that it disseminated. The humming whir of the great alternator rose gradually into a scream like the outcry of some angry thing. And then unexpectedly a shaft of pale lavender light shot out from the glowing hood and lost itself in the blackness of the midnight sky. Now appeared a wonderful and beautiful spectacle: immediately above the point where the rays disappeared into the ether hundreds of points of yellow fire suddenly sprang into being in the sky, darting hither and thither like fireflies, some moving slowly and others with such speed they appeared as even, luminous lines.

"*Les marionettes! Les marionettes!*" Marc cried trembling.

"Not at all! Not at all! They are meteorites!" answered Bennie, entirely engrossed in the scientific phase of the matter and forgetting that he did not speak the other's language. "Space is jammed full of meteoric dust. The larger particles, which strike our atmosphere and which ignite by friction, form shooting stars. The Ray—the Lavender Ray—reaching out into the most distant regions of space meets them in countless numbers and disintegrates them, surrounding them with glowing atmospheres. By George, though, if he starts in playing the Ray upon that cliff we've got to stand from under! Look here, boys," he shouted, "stuff something in your ears." He seized his handkerchief, tore it apart, and, making two plugs, thrust them into the openings of his ears as far as the drums. The others in wonderment followed his example.

"He's going to rock the earth!" cried Bennie Hooker. "He's going to rock the earth again!"

Slowly the Lavender Ray swung through the ether, followed by its millions of meteorites, dipping downward toward the northern side of the valley and sinking ever lower and lower toward the cliff. Bennie threw himself flat on his stomach upon the ridge, pressing his hands to his ears, and the others, feeling that something terrible was going to happen, followed his example. Nearer and nearer toward the ridge dropped the Ray. Bennie held his breath. Another instant and there came a blinding splash of yellow light, a crash like thunder, and a roar that seemed to tear the mountain from its base. The earth shook. Into the zenith sprang a flame of incandescent vapour a mile in height. The tumult increased. Vivid blue flashes of lightning shot out from the spot upon which the Ray played. The air was filled with thunderings, and the ground beneath them rose and fell and swung from side to side. Then came a mighty wind, nay, a cyclone, and gravel and broken branches fell upon them, and suffocating clouds of dust filled their eyes and shut out from time to time what was occurring in the valley. The face of the cliff glowed like the interior of a furnace, and the blazing yellow blast of glowing helium shot over their heads and off into space, making the night sky light as day.

For a moment they all lay stunned and sightless. Then the discharge appeared to diminish both in volume and in intensity. The air cleared somewhat and the ground no longer trembled. The burst of flame slowly subsided, like a fountain that is being gradually turned off. Either the Ring man wasn't going to rock the earth or he had lost control of his machinery.

Something was clearly going wrong. Showers of sparks fell from the hood and occasionally huge glowing masses of molten metal dropped from it. And now the Lavender Ray began slowly to sweep down the face of the cliff; and the yellow blast of helium gradually faded away until it was scarcely visible. The roar of the alternator died down, first to a hum and then to a purr.

"Something's busted," thought Bennie, "and he's shut it off."

The Ray had now reached the bottom of the cliff and was sweeping across the ground toward the base of the tower, its path being marked by a small travelling volcano that hurled its smoke and steam high into the air. It was evident to Bennie that the hood of the tower was slowly turning over, and that the now fast-fading Ray would presently play upon its base and the adjacent cupola in which the master of the Ring was probably attempting to control his recalcitrant machinery.

And then Bennie lost consciousness.

A splash of rain. He awoke, and found himself lying by the barbed-wire fence in the graying light of dawn. His muscles were stiff and sore, but he felt a strange sense of exhilaration. A mist was driving across the valley and enshrouding the scene of the night's debacle. Through the rain gusts he could see, still standing, the wreck of the tower, with a fragment of melted inductor drooping from its apex—and a long way off the Ring. The base of the tower and its surroundings were lost in mist. He crawled to his knees and looked about him for Marc and Edouard, but they had disappeared. His field glasses lay beside him, and he picked them up and raised himself to his feet. Like stout Cortés, silent upon his peak in Darien, he surveyed the Pacific of his dreams. For the Ring was still there! Pax might be annihilated, his machinery destroyed, but the secret remained—and it was his, Bennie Hooker's, of Appian Way, Cambridge, Massachusetts! In his excitement, in getting over the fence he tore a jagged hole in what was left of his sporting suit, but in a moment more he was scrambling down the ridge into the ravine.

He found it no easy task to climb down the jagged face of the cliff, but twenty minutes of stiff work landed him in the valley and within a thousand yards of the stark remains of the tower. Between where he stood and the devastation caused by the culminating explosion of the night before, the surface of the earth showed the customary ledges of barren rock, the scraggy scattering of firs, and stretches of moss with which he had become so familiar. Behind him the monorail, springing into space from the crest of the hill, ended in the dangling wreckage of a trestle which evidently had terminated in a station, now vanished, near the tower. From his point of observation little of the results of the upheaval was noticeable except the débris, which lay in a film of shattered rock and gravel over the surface of the ground, but as he ran toward the tower the damage caused by the Ray quickly became apparent.

At the distance of two hundred yards from the base he paused astounded. Why anything of the tower remained at all was a mystery, explicable only by reason of the skeletonlike character of its construction. All about it the surface had been rent as by an earthquake, and save for a fragment of the dome or bombproof all trace of buildings had disappeared. A glistening lake of leperous-like molten lead lay in the centre of the crater, strangely iridescent. A broad path of destruction, fifty yards or so in width, led from the scene of the disruption to the precipice against which the Ray had played. The face of the cliff itself seemed covered with a white coating or powder which gave it a ghostly sheen. Moreover, the rain had turned to snow and already the entire aspect of the valley had changed.

Bennie stood wonderingly on the edge of this inferno. He was cold, famished, horror-stricken. Like a flash in a pan the mechanism which had rocked the earth and dislocated its axis had blown out; and there was now nothing left to tell the story, for its inventor had flashed out with it into eternity. At his very feet a conscious human being, only twelve short hours before, had by virtue of his stupendous brain been able to generate and control a force capable of destroying the planet itself, and now——! He was gone! It was all gone! Unless somewhere hard by was hovering amid the whirling snowflakes that which might be his soul. But Pax would send no more messages! Bennie's journey had gone for naught. He had arrived just too late to talk it all over with his fellow-scientist, and discuss those little improvements on Hiroshito's theory. Pax was dead!

He sat down wearily, noticing for the first time that his ears pained him. In his depression and excitement he had totally forgotten the Ring. He wondered how he was ever going to get back to Cambridge. And then as he raised his hand to adjust his Glengarry he saw it awaiting him—unscathed. Far to the westward it rested snugly in its gigantic nest of crossbeams, like the head of some colossal decapitated Chinese mandarin. With an involuntary shout he started running down the valley, heedless of his steps. Nearer and higher loomed the steel trestlework upon which rested the giant engine. Panting, he blindly stumbled on, mindful only of the momentous fact that Pax's secret was not lost.

Fifty feet above the ground, supported upon a cylindrical trestle of steel girders, rested the body of the car, constructed of aluminum plates in the form of an anchor ring some seventy-five feet in diameter, while over the circular structure of the Ring itself rose a skeleton tower like a tripod, carrying at its summit a huge metal device shaped like a thimble, the open mouth of which pointed downward through the open centre of the machine. Obviously this must be the tractor or radiant engine. There, too, swung far out from the side of the ring on a framework of steel, was the thermic inductor which had played the disintegrating Ray upon the Atlas Mountains and the great cannon of Von Heckmann. The whole affair resembled nothing which he had ever conceived of either in the air, the earth, or the waters under the earth, the bizarre invention of a superhuman mind. It seemed as firmly anchored and as immovable as the Eiffel Tower, and yet Bennie knew that the thing could lift itself into the air and sail off like a ball of thistledown before a breeze. He knew that it could do it, for he had seen it with his own eyes.

A few steps more brought him into the centre of the circle of steel girders which supported the landing stage. Here the surface of the earth at his feet had been completely denuded and the underlying rock exposed, evidently by some artificial action, the downward blast of gas from the tractor. Even the rock itself had been seared by the discharge; little furrows worn smooth as if by a mountain torrent radiating in all directions from the central point. More than anything it reminded Bennie of the surface of a meteorite, polished and scarred by its rush through the atmosphere. He paused, filled with a kind of awe. The most wonderful engine of all time waited his inspection. The great secret was his alone. The inventor and his associates had been wiped out of existence in a flash, and the Flying Ring was his by every right of treasure trove. In the heart of the Labrador wilderness Prof. Benjamin Hooker of Cambridge, Massachusetts, gave an exultant shout, threw off his coat, and swarmed up the steel ladder leading to the landing stage.

He had ascended about halfway when a voice echoed among the girders. A red face was peering down at him over the edge of the platform.

"Hello!" said the face. "I'm all right, I guess."

Bennie gripped tight hold of the ladder, stiff with fear. He thought first of jumping down, changed his mind, and, shutting his eyes, continued automatically climbing up the ladder.

Then a hand gripped him under the arm and gave him a lift on to the level floor of the platform. He steadied himself and opened his eyes. Before him stood a man in blue overalls, under whose forehead, burned bright red by the Labrador sun, a pair of blue eyes looked out vaguely. The man appeared to be waiting for the visitor to make the next move. "Good morning," said Bennie, sparring for time. "Well"—he hesitated—"where were you when it happened?"

The man looked at him stupidly. "What?" he mumbled. "I—I don't seem to remember. You see—I was in—the condenser room building up the charge—for to-morrow—I mean to-day—sixty thousand volts at the terminals, and the fluid clearing up. I guess I looked out of the window a minute—to see—the fireworks—and then—somehow—I was out on the platform." He shaded his eyes and looked off down the valley at the half-shattered, wrecked tower. "The wind and the smoke!" he muttered. "The wind and the smoke—and the dust in my eyes—and now it's all gone to hell! But I guess everything's all right now, if you want to fly." He touched his cap automatically. "We can start whenever you are ready, sir. You see I thought you were gone, too! That would have been a mess! I'm sure you can handle the balancer without Perkins. Poor old Perk! And Hoskins—and the others. All gone, by God! All wiped out! Only me and you left, sir!" He laughed hysterically.

"Bats in his belfry!" thought Bennie. "Something hit him!"

Slowly it came over him that the half-stunned creature thought that he, Bennie Hooker, was Pax, the Master of the World!

He took the fellow by the arm. "Come on inside," he said. A plan had already formulated itself in his brain. Even as he was the man might be able to go through his customary duties in handling the Ring. It was not impossible. He had heard of such things, and the thought of the long marches over the frozen barrens and the perilous canoe trip down the coast, contrasted with a swift rush for an hour or two through the sunlit air, gave the professor the courage which might not have availed him otherwise. At the top of a short ladder a trapdoor opened inward, and Bennie found himself in a small compartment scarcely large enough to turn around in, from which a second door opened into the body of the Ring proper.

"It's all right—to-day," said the man hesitatingly. "I fixed—the air-lock—yesterday, sir. The leak—was here—at the hinge—but it's quite tight—now." He pointed at the door.

"Good," remarked Bennie. "I'll look around and see how things are."

This seemed to him to be eminently safe—and allowing for a program of investigation absolutely essential at the moment. Once he could master the secret of the Ring and be sure that the part of the fellow's brain which controlled the performance of his customary duties had not been injured by the shock of the night before, it might be possible to carry out the daring project which had suggested itself.

Passing through the inner door of the air-lock he entered the chart room of the Ring, followed stumblingly by his companion. It was warm and cozy; the first warmth Hooker had experienced for nearly a month. It made him feel faint, and he dropped into an armchair and pulled off his Glengarry. The survivor of the explosion, standing awkwardly at his side, fumbled with his cap. Ever and anon he rubbed his head.

Bennie sank back into the cushions and looked about him. On the opposite wall hung a map of the world on Mercator's Projection, and from a spot in Northern Labrador red lines radiated in all directions, which formed great curved loops, returning to the starting-point.

"The flights of the Ring," thought Bennie. "There's the one where they busted the Atlas Mountains," following with his eyes the crimson thread which ran diagonally across the Atlantic, traversed Spain and the Mediterranean, and circling in a narrow loop over the coast of Northern Africa turned back into its original track. Visions came to him of guiding the car for an afternoon jaunt across the Sahara, the gloomy forests of the Congo, into the Antarctic, and thence home in time for afternoon tea, via the Easter Islands, Hawaii, and Alaska. But why stop there? What was to prevent a trip to the moon? Or Mars? Or for that matter into the unknown realms outside the solar system—the fourth dimension, perhaps—or even the fifth dimension——

"Excuse me," said the machinist suddenly, "I just forgot—whether you take—cigars or cigarettes. You see I only acted as—table orderly—once—when Smith had that sprain." His hands moved uncertainly on the shelves, beyond the map. The heart of Professor Hooker leaped.

"Cigars!" he almost shouted.

The man found a box of Havanas and struck a match.

The bliss of it! And if there was tobacco there must be food and drink as well. He began to feel strangely exhilarated. But how to handle the man beside him? Pax would certainly never ask the questions that he wished to ask. He smoked rapidly, thinking hard. Of course he might pretend that he, too, had forgotten things. And at first this seemed to be the only way out of the difficulty. Then he had an inspiration.

"Look here," he remarked, rather severely. "Something's happened to you. You say you've forgotten what occurred yesterday? How do I know but you have forgotten everything you ever knew? You remember your name?"

"My name, sir?" The man laughed in a foolish fashion. "Why—of course I remember—my name. I wouldn't—be likely—to forget—that: Atterbury—I'm Atterbury—electrician of the *Chimaera*." And he drew himself up.

"That's all right," said Bennie, "but what were we doing yesterday? What is the very last thing that you can go back to?"

The man wrinkled his forehead. "The last thing? Why, sir, you told us you were going—to turn over the pole a bit—and freeze up Europe. I was up here—loading the condenser—when you cut me off from the alternator. I opened the switch—and put on the electrometer to see—if we had enough. Next—everything was clouded, and I went—over to the window to see—what was going on."

"Yes," commented Bennie approvingly, "all right so far. What happened then?"

"Why, after that, sir, after that, there was the Ray of course, and er—I don't seem to remember—oh, yes, a short circuit—and I ran—out on the platform—forgot all about the danger! After that, everything's confused. It's like a dream. Your coming up—the ladder—seemed—to wake me up." The machinist smiled sheepishly.

The plan was working well. Professor Hooker was learning things fast.

"Do you think that the two of us can fly the *Chimaera* south again?" he asked, inspecting the map.

"Why not?" answered Atterbury. "The balancer is working—better now—and—doesn't take—much attention—and you can lay the course—and manage

—the landing. I was going to put a fresh uranium cylinder in the tractor this morning—but I—forgot."

"There you go, forgetting again!" growled Bennie, realizing that his only excuse for asking questions hung on this fiction. And there were many, many more questions that he must ask before he would be able to fly. "You don't seem quite right in your coco this morning, Atterbury," he said. "I think we'll look things over a bit—the condenser first."

"Very well, sir." Atterbury turned and groped his way through a doorway, and they passed first into what appeared to be a storage-battery room. Huge glass tanks filled with amber-coloured fluid, in which numerous parallel plates were supported, lined the walls from floor to ceiling.

An ammeter on the wall caught Bennie's attention. "Weston Direct Reading A. C. Ammeter," he read on the dial. Alternate current! What were they doing with an alternating current in the storage-battery room? His eyes followed the wires along the wall. Yes, they ran to the terminals of the battery. It dawned upon him that there might be something here undreamed of in electrical engineering—a storage battery for an alternating current!

The electrician closed a row of switches, brought the two polished brass spheres of the discharger within striking distance, and instantly a blinding current of sparks roared between the terminals. He had been right. This battery not only was charged by an alternating current, but delivered one of high potential. He peered into the cells, racking his brain for an explanation.

"Atterbury," said he meditatively, "did I ever tell you why they do that?"

"Yes," answered the man. "You—told me—once. The two metals—in the electrolyte—come down—on the plates—in alternate films—as—the current changes direction. But you never told me—what the electrolyte was—I don't suppose—you—would be willing to now, would you?"

"H'm," said Bennie, "some time, maybe."

But this cue was all that he required. A clever scheme! Pax had formed layers of molecular thickness of two different metals in alternation by the to-and-fro swing of his charging current. When the battery discharged the metals went into solution, each plate becoming alternately positive and negative. He wondered what Pax had used for an electrolyte that enabled him to get a metallic deposit at each electrode. And he wondered also why the metals did not alloy. But it would not do for him to linger too long over a mere detail of equipment. And he turned away to continue his tour of inspection, a tour which occupied most of the morning, and during which he found a well-stocked gallery and made himself a cup of coffee. *

But the more he learned about the mechanism of the Ring the greater became his misgivings about undertaking the return journey alone with Atterbury

---

* He even climbed with Atterbury to the very summit of the tractor, where he discovered that his original guess had been correct and that the car rose from the earth rocket fashion, due to the back pressure of the radiant discharge from a massive cylinder of uranium contained in the tractor. Against this block played a disintegrating ray from a small thermic inductor, the inner construction of which he was not able to determine, although it was obviously different from his own, and the coils were wound in a curious manner which he did not understand. There might be something in Hiroshito's theory after all. The cylinder of the tractor pointed directly downward so that the blast was discharged through the very centre of the Ring, but it could be swung through a small angle in any direction, and by means of this slight deflection the horizontal motion of the machine secured. Perhaps the most interesting feature of the mechanism was that the Ring appeared to have automatic stability, for the angle of the direction in which the tractor was pointed was controlled not only by a pair of gyroscopes which kept the Ring on an even keel, but also by a manometric valve causing it to fly at a fixed height above the earth's surface. Should it start to rise, the diminished pressure of the atmosphere operating on the valve swung the tractor more to one side, and the horizontal acceleration was thus increased at the expense of the vertical.

through the air. If they were to go, the start must be made within a few days, for the condenser held its charge but a comparatively short time, and its energy was necessary for starting the Ring. When freshly charged it supplied current for the thermic inductor for nearly three minutes, but the metallic films, deposited on the plates, dissolved slowly in the fluid, and after three or four days there remained only enough for a thirty-second run, hardly enough to lift the Ring from the earth. Once in the air, the downward blast from the tractor operated a turbine alternator mounted on a skeleton framework at the centre of the Ring, and the current supplied by this machine enabled the Ring to continue its flight indefinitely, or until the cylinder of uranium was completely disintegrated.

Yet to trek back over the route by which he had come appeared to be equally impossible. There was little likelihood that the two Indians would return; they were probably already thirty miles on their way back to the coast. If only he could get word to Thornton or some of those chaps at Washington they might send a relief expedition! But a ship would be weeks in getting to the coast, and how could he live in the meantime? There were provisions for only a few days in the Ring, and the storehouse in the valley had been wiped out of existence. Only an aeroplane could do the trick. And then he thought of Burke, his classmate—Burke who had devoted his life to heavier-than-air machines, and who, since his memorable flight across the Atlantic in the *Stormy Petrol*, had been a national hero. Burke could reach him in ten hours, but how could *he* reach Burke? In the heart of the frozen wilderness of Labrador he might as well be on another planet, as far as communication with the civilized world was concerned.

A burst of sunlight shot through the window and formed an oval patch on the floor at his feet. The weather was clearing. He went out upon the platform. Patches of blue sky appeared overhead. As he gazed disconsolately across the valley toward the tower, his eye caught the glisten of something high in the air. From the top of the wreckage five thin shining lines ran parallel across the sky and disappeared in a small cloud which hung low over the face of the cliff.

"The antennæ!" exclaimed Bennie. "A wireless to Burke." Burke would come; he knew Burke. A thousand miles overland was nothing to him. Hadn't he wagered five thousand dollars at the club that he would fly to the pole and bring back Peary's flag—with no takers? Why, Burke would take him home with as little trouble as a taxicab. And then, aghast, he remembered the complete destruction in the valley. The wireless plant had gone with the rest. He ran back into the chart room and called Atterbury.

"Can we get off a message to Washington?" he demanded. "The wires are still up, and we have the condenser."

"We might, sir, if it's not—a long one, though you've always said there was danger in running the engine with the car bolted down. We did it the time the big machine burnt out a coil. I can throw —a wire—over the antennæ with a rocket—and join up—with the turbine machine. It will increase—our wave length, but they ought to pick us up."

"We'll try it, anyway," announced Bennie.

He inspected the chart and measured the distance in an airline from Boston to the point where the red lines converged. It was a trifle less than the distance between Boston and Chicago. Burke had done that in nine hours on the trial trip of his trans-Atlantic monoplane. If the machine was in order and Burke started in the morning he would be with them by sunset, if he didn't get lost. But Bennie knew that Burke could drive his machine by dead reckoning and strike within a few leagues of a target a thousand miles away.

A muffled roar outside interrupted his musings, and running out on the platform again he found Atterbury attaching the cord of the aluminum ribbon, which the rocket had carried up and over the antennæ, to one of the brush bars of the alternator.

"Nearly ready, sir," he said. "We'd best—lock the storm bolts—to hold her down—in case we have —to crowd on the power. We've got to use— pretty near the full lift—to get the alternator up—to the proper speed."

A chill ran down Bennie's spine. They were going to start the engine! In a moment he would be within twenty feet of a blast of disintegration products capable of lifting the whole machine into the air, and it was to be started at his command, after he had worked and pottered for two years with a thermic inductor the size of a thimble! He felt as he used to feel before taking a high dive, or as he imagined a soldier feels when about to go under fire for the first time. How would it turn out? Was he taking too much responsibility, and was Atterbury counting on him for the management of details? He felt singularly helpless as he reëntered the chart room to compose his message.

He turned on the electric lamp which hung over the desk, for in the fast-gathering dusk the interior of the Ring was in almost total darkness. How should his message read? It must be brief: it must tell the story, and, above all, it must be compelling.

He was joined by the electrician.

"I think—we are all—ready now," stammered the latter. "What will you send, sir?"

Bennie handed him a scrap of yellow paper, and Atterbury put on a pair of dark amber glasses, to protect his eyes from the light of the spark.

"*Thornton, Naval Observatory, Washington:*

"Stranded fifty-four thirty-eight north, seventy-four eighteen west. Have the Ring machine. Ask Burke come immediately. Life and death matter.
"B. HOOKER."

THE MAN WHO ROCKED THE EARTH

Atterbury read the message and then gazed blankly at Hooker.

"I—don't—understand," he said.

"Never mind, send it. I'll explain later." Together they went into the condenser room.

Atterbury mechanically pushed the brass balls in contact, shoved a bundle of iron wires halfway through the core of a great coil, and closed a switch. A humming sound filled the air, and a few seconds later a glow of yellow light came in through the window. A cone of luminous vapour was shooting downward through the centre of the Ring from the tractor. At first it was soft and nebulous, but it increased rapidly in brilliancy, and a dull roar, like that of a waterfall, added itself to the hum of the alternating current in the wires. And now a third sound came to his ears, the note of the turbine, low at first, but gradually rising like the scream of a siren, and the floor of the Ring beneath his feet throbbed with the vibration.

Bennie forgot the dynamometer, forgot his message to Burke, was conscious only that he had wakened a sleeping volcano. Then came the crack of the sparks, and the room seemed filled with the glare of the blue lightning, for Atterbury, with his telephones at his ears, staring through his yellow glasses, was sending out the call for the Naval Observatory.

"NAA—NAA—P—A—X."

Over and over again he sent the call, while in the meantime the condenser built up its charge from the overflow of current from the turbine generator. Then the electrician opened a switch, and the roar outside diminished and finally ceased.

"We can't listen—with the tractor running," he fretted. "The static—from the discharge—would tear—our detector—to pieces." He threw in the receiving instrument. For a few moments the telephones spoke only the whisperings of the arctic aurora, and then suddenly the faint cry of the answering spark was heard. Bennie watched the words as the electrician's pencil scrawled along on the paper.

"Waiting for you. Why don't you send? N. A. A."

"They must have—called us before—while the discharge—was running down," muttered Atterbury. "I think we can send—with the condenser—now."

He picked up the scrap of yellow paper, read it over, and threw out into space the message which he did not understand.

THE MAN WHO ROCKED THE EARTH

"O. K. Wait. Thornton," came in reply.

Two hours later came a second message:

"P—A—X. Burke starts at daybreak. Expects reach you by nine P. M. Asks you to show large beacon fire if possible.
"THORNTON, N. A. A."

"Hurrah!" cried Bennie. "Good for Burke! Atterbury, we're saved—saved, do you hear! Go to bed now and don't ask any questions. And say, before you go see if you can find me a glass of brandy."

It was decided that Burke must land on the plateau above the cliff, and here the material for the fire was collected. There was little enough of it and it was hard work carrying the oil up the steep trail. At times Bennie was almost in despair.

"It won't burn half an hour," said he, surveying the pile. "And we ought to be able to keep it going all night. There's plenty of stuff in the valley, but we can't have him come down there, with the tower, the antennæ, and all the rest of the mess."

"We might—show him—the big Ray," ventured Atterbury. "The thing—can be pointed up—and I can—keep the turbine running. You can start—the fire—as soon as you—hear his motors—and I'll shut down—as soon as I see your fire."

"Good idea!" agreed Bennie. "Only don't run continuously. Show the Ray for a minute every quarter of an hour, and on no account start up after you see the fire. If he thought the vertical beam was a searchlight and flew through it——" Bennie shuddered at the thought of Burke driving his aeroplane through the Ray that had shattered the Atlas Mountains.

So it was arranged. Half an hour after sunset Atterbury shut himself up in the Ring, and while Bennie climbed the trail leading to his post on the plateau, he heard the creaking of the great inductor as it slowly turned on its trunions.

It was pitch dark by the time he reached the pitifully small pile of brush which they had collected, and he poured some of the oil over it and sat down, drawing a blanket around his shoulders. He felt very much alone. Suppose the inductor failed to work? Suppose Atterbury turned the Ray on him? Suppose. . . . But his musings were shattered by a noise from the valley, a sound like that of escaping steam, and a moment later the Lavender Ray shot up

THE MAN WHO ROCKED THE EARTH 213

toward the zenith. Bennie lay on his back and watched it, mindful of the night before the last when he had watched the Ray from the tower descending upon the cliff. He wondered if he should see any meteorites kindle in its path, but nothing appeared and the Ray died down, leaving everything in darkness again. Fifteen minutes passed and again the ghostly beam shot up into the night sky. Bennie looked at his watch. It was nearly half-past eight. The cold made him sleepy. He drew the blanket about him. . . .

Two hours later through his half-dreams he caught the faint sound for which he had been listening. At first he was not sure. It might be the turbine alternator of the Ring running by its own inertia for some time after the discharge had ceased. But no, it was growing louder momentarily, and appeared to come from high up in the air. Now it died away to nothingness, and now it swelled in volume, and again died away. But at each subsequent recurrence it was louder than before. There was no longer any doubt. Burke was coming! It was time to start the brush pile. He lit match after match, only for the wind to blow them out. Yet all the time the machine in the air was coming nearer, the roar of its twin engines beating on the stillness of the Labrador night. In despair Bennie threw himself flat on his face by the brush pile and made a tent of the blanket, under which he at last succeeded in starting a blaze among the oil-soaked twigs. Then he pushed the half-empty keg into the fire, arose and stared up at the sky.

The machine was somewhere directly above him—just where he could not say. Presently the motors stopped. He shouted feebly, running up and down with his eyes turned skyward, and several times nearly fell into the fire. He wondered why it didn't appear. It seemed hours since the motors stopped! Then unexpectedly against the black background of the sky the great wings of the machine appeared, illuminated on their underside by the light of the fire. Silently it swung around on its descending spiral, instantly to be swallowed up in the darkness again, a moment later reappearing from the opposite direction, this time low down and headed straight for him. He jumped hastily to one side and fell flat. The machine grounded, rose once or twice as it ran along the ground, and came to a stop twenty yards from the fire. A man climbed out, slowly removed

THE MAN WHO ROCKED THE EARTH 215

his goggles, and shook himself. Bennie scrambled to his feet and ran forward waving his hat.

"Well, Hooker!" remarked the man. "What th' hell are you doing *here?* You sure have some searchlight!"

How Hooker and Burke, under the guidance of Atterbury, who gradually regained his normal mental status, explored and charted the valley of the Ring is strictly no part of this tale which deals solely with the end of War upon the Earth. But next day, after several hours of excavation among the débris of the smelter, where Pax had extracted his uranium from the pitch blend mined at the cliff, they uncovered eight cylinders of the precious metal weighing about one hundred pounds apiece—the fuel of the Flying Ring. Now they were safe. Nay, more: universal space was theirs to traffic in.

Curious as to the reason why Pax had isolated himself in this frozen wilderness, they next examined the high cliffs which shut in the valley on the west and against the almost perpendicular walls of which he had played the Lavender Ray. These cliffs proved, as Bennie had already suspected, to be a gigantic outcrop of pitchblend or black oxide of uranium. He estimated that nature had stored more uranium in but one of the abutments of this cliff than in all the known mines of the entire world. This radioactive mountain was the fulcrum by which this modern Archimedes had moved the earth. The vast amount of matter disintegrated by the Ray and thrown off into space with a velocity a thousandfold greater than the blast of a siege gun produced a back pressure or recoil against the face of the cliff, which thus became the "thrust block" of the force which had slowed down the period of the earth's rotation.

The day of the start dawned with a blazing sun. From the landing stage of the Ring Bennie could see stretching away to the east, west, and south, the interminable plains, dotted with firs, which had formed the natural barrier to the previous discovery of Pax's secret. Overhead the dome of the sky fitted the horizon like an enormous shell—a shell which, with a thrill, he realized that he could crack and escape from, like a fledgling ready for its first flight. And yet in this moment of triumph little Bennie Hooker felt the qualm which must inevitably come to those who take their lives in their hands. An hour and he would be either soaring Phoebus-like toward the south, or lying crushed and mangled within a tangled mass of wreckage. Even here in this desolate waste life seemed sweet, and he had much, so much to do. Wasn't it, after all, a crazy thing to try to navigate the complicated mechanism back to civilization? Yet something told him that unless he put his fate to the test now he would never return. He had the utmost confidence in Burke—he might never be able to secure his services again—no, it was now or never. He entered the airlock, closing and bolting the door, and passed on into the chart room.

At all events, he thought, they were no worse off than Pax when he had made his first trial flight, and they were working with a proven machine, tuned to its fullest efficiency, and one which apparently possessed automatic stability. Atterbury had gone to the condenser room and was waiting for the order to start, while Burke was making the final adjustment of the gyroscopes which would put the Ring on its predetermined course. He came through the door and joined Bennie.

"Hooker," he said, "we're sure going to have some experience. If I can keep her from turning over, I think I can manage her. The trouble will come when we slant the tractor. I'm not sure how much depends on the atmospheric valve, and how much on me. Things may happen quickly. If we turn over we're done for."

He held out his hand to Bennie, who gripped it tremulously.

"Well," remarked the aviator, tossing away his cigarette, "we might as well die now as any time!"

He walked swiftly over to the speaking-tube which communicated with the condenser room and blew sharply into it.

"Let her go, *Gallagher!*" he directed.

"My God!" ejaculated Bennie. "Wait a second, can't you?"

But it was too late. He grabbed the rail, trembling. A humming sound filled the air, and the gyroscopes slowly began to revolve. He looked up through the window at the tractor, from which shot streaks of pale vapour with a noise like escaping steam. Somehow it seemed alive.

The Ring was throbbing as if it, too, was impreg-

THE MAN WHO ROCKED THE EARTH 219

nated with life. The discharge of the tractor had risen to a muffled roar. Shaking all over, Bennie crossed to the inside window and looked across the inner space of the Ring. As yet the yellow glow of the discharge was scarcely visible, but the steel sides of the Ring danced and quivered, undulating in waves, and, as the intensity of the blast increased and the turbine commenced to revolve, everything outside went suddenly blurred and indistinct.

Dropping to his knees, Bennie looked down through the observation window in the floor. A blinding cloud of yellow dust was driving out and away from the base of the landing stage in the form of a gigantic ring. The earth at their feet was hidden in whirls of vapour; and ripples of light and shade chased each other outward in all directions, like shadows on the bottom of a sandy pond rippled by a breeze. It made him dizzy to look down there, and he arose from the window. Burke stood grimly at the control, unmindful of his associate. Bennie crossed to the other side, and as he passed the gyroscopes, the air from the swiftly spinning discs blew back his hair. He could see nothing through the tumult that roared down through the centre of the Ring, like a

Niagara of hot steam shot through with a pale yellow phosphorescent light. The floor quivered under his feet, and ominous creaking and snapping sounds reverberated through the outer shell, as the steel girders of the landing stage were gradually relieved of its weight. Just as it seemed to him that everything was going to pieces, suddenly there was silence, save for the purr of the machinery, and Bennie felt his knees sink under him.

"We're off!" cried Burke. "Watch out!"

The floor swayed as the Ring, lifted by the tractor, swung to and fro like a pendulum. Bennie threw himself upon his stomach. The earth was dropping away from them like a stone. He felt a sickening sensation.

"Two thousand feet already," gasped Burke. "The atmospheric valve is set for five thousand. I'll make it ten! It will give us more room to recover in —if anything—goes wrong!"

He gave the knob another half turn and laid his hand lightly on the lever which controlled the movements of the tractor. Bennie, flattened against the window, gazed below. The great dust ring showed indistinctly through a blue haze no longer directly

THE MAN WHO ROCKED THE EARTH

beneath them, but a quarter of a mile to the north. Evidently they were not rising vertically.

The valley of the Ring looked like a black crack in a greenish-gray desert of rock and moss, the landing stage like a tiny bird's nest. The floor of the car moved slightly from side to side. Burke's face had gone gray, and he crouched unsteadily, one hand gripping a steel bracket on the wall.

"My Lord!" he mumbled with dry lips. "My Lord!"

Bennie, momentarily expecting annihilation, crawled on all fours to Burke's side.

The needle of the manometer indicated nine thousand five hundred feet, and was rapidly nearing the next division. Suddenly Burke felt the lever move slowly under his hand as though operated by some outside intelligence, and at the same moment the axis of one gyroscope swung slowly in a horizontal plane through an angle of nearly ninety degrees, while that of the other dipped slightly from the vertical. Both men had a ghastly feeling that the ghost of Pax had somehow returned and assumed control of the car. Bennie rotated the map under the gyroscope until the fine black line on the dial again lay across their destination. Then he crept back to his window again. The earth, far below and dimly visible, was sliding slowly northward, and the dust ring which marked their starting-point now lay as a flattened ellipse on the distant horizon. Beneath and behind them in their flight trailed a thin streak of pale bluish fog—the wake of the Flying Ring.

They were now searing the atmosphere at a height of nearly two miles, and the car was flying on a firm and even keel. There was no sound save the dull roar of the tractor and a slight humming from the vibration of the light steel cables. Bennie no longer felt any disagreeable sensation. A strange detachment possessed him. Dark forests, lakes, and a mighty river appeared to the south—the Moisie—and they followed it as a fishhawk might have done, until the wilderness broke away before them and they saw the broad reach of the St. Lawrence streaked with the smoke of ocean liners.

And then he lost control of himself for the first time and sobbed like a woman—not from fear, nor weariness, nor excitement, but for joy—the joy of the true scientist who has sought the truth and found it, has achieved that for mankind which but for him it would have lacked, perchance, forever. And he looked up at Burke and smiled.

The latter nodded.

"Yes," he remarked prosaically, "this is sure a little bit of all right! All to the good!"

EPILOGUE

MEANWHILE, during the weeks that Hooker had been engaged in finding the valley of the Ring, unbelievable things had happened in world politics. In spite of the fact that Pax, having decreed the shifting of the Pole and the transformation of Central Europe into the Arctic zone, had refused further communication with mankind, all the nations—and none more zealously than the German Republic—had proceeded immediately to withdraw their armies within their own borders, and under the personal supervision of a General Commission to destroy all their armaments and munitions of war. The lyddite bombs, manufactured in vast quantities by the Krupps for the Relay Gun and all other high explosives, were used to demolish the fortresses upon every frontier of Europe. The contents of every arsenal was loaded upon barges and sunk in mid-Atlantic. And every form of military organization, rank, service, and even uniform, was abolished throughout the world.

A coalition of nations was formed under a single general government, known as the United States of Europe, which in coöperation with the United States of North and South America, of Asia, and of Africa, arranged for an annual world congress at The Hague, and which enforced its decrees by means of an International Police. In effect all the inhabitants of the globe came under a single control, as far as language and geographical boundaries would permit. Each state enforced local laws, but all were obedient to the higher law—the Law of Humanity—which was uniform through the earth. If an individual offended against the law of one nation, he was held to have offended against all, and was dealt with as such. The international police needed no treaties of extradition. The New York embezzler who fled to Nairobi was sent back as a matter of course without delay.

Any man was free to go and live where he chose, to manufacture, buy, and sell as he saw fit. And, because the fear and shadow of war were removed, the nations grew rich beyond the imagination of men; great hospitals and research laboratories, universities, schools, and kindergartens, opera houses, theatres, and gardens of every sort sprang up everywhere, paid for no one quite knew how. The nations ceased to build dreadnoughts, and instead used the money to send great troops of children with the teachers travelling over the world. It was against the law to own or manufacture any weapon that could be used to take human life. And because the nations had nothing to fear from one another, and because there were no scheming diplomatists and bureaucrats to make a living out of imaginary antagonisms, people forgot that they were French or German or Russian or English, just as the people of the United States of America had long before practically disregarded the fact that they came from Ohio or Oregon or Connecticut or Nevada. Russians with weak throats went to live in Italy as a matter of course, and Spaniards who liked German cooking settled in München.

All this, of course, did not happen at once, but came about quite naturally after the abolition of war. And after it had been done, everybody wondered why it had not been done ten centuries before; and people became so interested in destroying all the relics of

THE MAN WHO ROCKED THE EARTH 227

that despicable employment, warfare, that they almost forgot that the Man Who Rocked the Earth had threatened that he would shift the axis of the globe. So that when the day fixed by him came and everything remained just as it always had been—and everybody still wore linen-mesh underwear in Strassburg and flannels in Archangel—nobody thought very much about it, or commented on the fact that the Flying Ring was no longer to be seen. And the only real difference was that you could take a P. & O. steamer at Marseilles and buy a through ticket to Tasili Ahaggar—if you wanted to go there—and that the shores of the Sahara became the Riviera of the world, crowded with health resorts and watering-places—so that Pax had not lived in vain, nor Thornton, nor Bill Hood, nor Bennie Hooker, nor any of them.

The whole thing is a matter of record, as it should be. The deliberations of Conference No. 2 broke up in a hubbub, just as Von Helmuth and Von Koenitz had intended, and the transcripts of their discussions proved to be not of the slightest scientific value. But in the files of the old War Department—now called the Department for the Alleviation of Poverty and

Human Suffering—can be read the messages interchanged between The Dictator of Human Destiny and the President of the United States, together with all the reports and observations relating thereto, including Professor Hooker's Report to the Smithsonian Institute of his journey to the valley of the Ring and what he found there. Only the secret of the Ring—of thermic induction and atomic disintegration—in short, of the Lavender Ray, is his by right of discovery, or treasure trove, or what you will, and so is his patent on Hooker's Space-Navigating Car, in which he afterward explored the solar system and the uttermost regions of the sidereal ether. But that shall be told hereafter.

THE END

THE COUNTRY LIFE PRESS, GARDEN CITY, NEW YORK

SCIENCE FICTION

An Arno Press Collection

FICTION

About, Edmond. **The Man with the Broken Ear.** 1872

Allen, Grant. **The British Barbarians:** A Hill-Top Novel. 1895

Arnold, Edwin L. **Lieut. Gullivar Jones:** His Vacation. 1905

Ash, Fenton. **A Trip to Mars.** 1909

Aubrey, Frank. **A Queen of Atlantis.** 1899

Bargone, Charles (Claude Farrere, pseud.). **Useless Hands.** [1926]

Beale, Charles Willing. **The Secret of the Earth.** 1899

Bell, Eric Temple (John Taine, pseud.). **Before the Dawn.** 1934

Benson, Robert Hugh. **Lord of the World.** 1908

Beresford, J. D. **The Hampdenshire Wonder.** 1911

Bradshaw, William R. **The Goddess of Atvatabar.** 1892

Capek, Karel. **Krakatit.** 1925

Chambers, Robert W. **The Gay Rebellion.** 1913

Colomb, P. et al. **The Great War of 189—.** 1893

Cook, William Wallace. **Adrift in the Unknown.** n.d.

Cummings, Ray. **The Man Who Mastered Time.** 1929

[DeMille, James]. **A Strange Manuscript Found in a Copper Cylinder.** 1888

Dixon, Thomas. **The Fall of a Nation:** A Sequel to the Birth of a Nation. 1916

England, George Allan. **The Golden Blight.** 1916

Fawcett, E. Douglas. **Hartmann the Anarchist.** 1893

Flammarion, Camille. **Omega:** The Last Days of the World. 1894

Grant, Robert et al. **The King's Men:** A Tale of To-Morrow. 1884

Grautoff, Ferdinand Heinrich (Parabellum, pseud.). **Banzai!** 1909

Graves, C. L. and E. V. Lucas. **The War of the Wenuses.** 1898

Greer, Tom. **A Modern Daedalus.** [1887]

Griffith, George. **A Honeymoon in Space.** 1901

Grousset, Paschal (A. Laurie, pseud.). **The Conquest of the Moon.** 1894

Haggard, H. Rider. **When the World Shook.** 1919

Hernaman-Johnson, F. **The Polyphemes.** 1906

Hyne, C. J. Cutcliffe. **Empire of the World.** [1910]

In The Future. [1875]

Jane, Fred T. **The Violet Flame.** 1899

Jefferies, Richard. **After London; Or, Wild England.** 1885

Le Queux, William. **The Great White Queen.** [1896]

London, Jack. **The Scarlet Plague.** 1915

Mitchell, John Ames. **Drowsy.** 1917

Morris, Ralph. **The Life and Astonishing Adventures of John Daniel.** 1751

Newcomb, Simon. **His Wisdom The Defender:** A Story. 1900

Paine, Albert Bigelow. **The Great White Way.** 1901

Pendray, Edward (Gawain Edwards, pseud.). **The Earth-Tube.** 1929

Reginald, R. and Douglas Menville. **Ancestral Voices:** An Anthology of Early Science Fiction. 1974

Russell, W. Clark. **The Frozen Pirate.** 2 vols. in 1. 1887

Shiel, M. P. **The Lord of the Sea.** 1901

Symmes, John Cleaves (Captain Adam Seaborn, pseud.). **Symzonia.** 1820

Train, Arthur and Robert W. Wood. **The Man Who Rocked the Earth.** 1915

Waterloo, Stanley. **The Story of Ab:** A Tale of the Time of the Cave Man. 1903

White, Stewart E. and Samuel H. Adams. **The Mystery.** 1907

Wicks, Mark. **To Mars Via the Moon.** 1911

Wright, Sydney Fowler. **Deluge: A Romance** and **Dawn.** 2 vols. in 1. 1928/1929

SCIENCE FICTION

NON-FICTION
Including Bibliographies,
Checklists and Literary Criticism

Aldiss, Brian and Harry Harrison. **SF Horizons.** 2 vols. in 1. 1964/1965

Amis, Kingsley. **New Maps of Hell.** 1960

Barnes, Myra. **Linguistics and Languages in Science Fiction-Fantasy.** 1974

Cockcroft, T. G. L. **Index to the Weird Fiction Magazines.** 2 vols. in 1 1962/1964

Cole, W. R. **A Checklist of Science-Fiction Anthologies.** 1964

Crawford, Joseph H. et al. **"333": A Bibliography of the Science-Fantasy Novel.** 1953

Day, Bradford M. **The Checklist of Fantastic Literature in Paperbound Books.** 1965

Day, Bradford M. **The Supplemental Checklist of Fantastic Literature.** 1963

Gove, Philip Babcock. **The Imaginary Voyage in Prose Fiction.** 1941

Green, Roger Lancelyn. **Into Other Worlds:** Space-Flight in Fiction, From Lucian to Lewis. 1958

Menville, Douglas. **A Historical and Critical Survey of the Science Fiction Film.** 1974

Reginald, R. **Contemporary Science Fiction Authors,** First Edition. 1970

Samuelson, David. **Visions of Tomorow:** Six Journeys from Outer to Inner Space. 1974